Saving Moirra's Heart

Suzan Tidsale

Cover design by: Seductive Designs
Copyright © 2014 Suzan Tisdale
All rights reserved.
ISBN-13: 978-1514273708

All rights reserved. This book or any portion thereof may not be reproduced or used in any manner whatsoever without the express written permission of the publisher except for the use of brief quotations in a book review.

DEDICATION

I want to thank the Guardians of Cridhe authors — Ceci Giltenan, Tarah Scott, Kate Robbins, Sue-Ellen Welfonder, Lily Baldwin and Kathryn Lynn Davis — for asking me to be a part of the beautiful *Highland Winds Collection*.

That is where the story you are about to read began, as a tiny idea in 2014, which blossomed into *Stealing Moirra's Heart*, and I continue with *Saving Moirra's Heart* today.

My Guardians of Cridhe sisters are some of the most talented, amazing women that I have ever had the pleasure of knowing or working with. Their never ending encouragement and support, has helped make me the woman I am today.

In addition to them, I want to also thank Tanya Anne Crosby and Kathryn LeVeque. All of these women helped me get through one of the darkest and saddest times of my entire life, the loss of my mother. Without these women in my life I seriously doubt I would have made it through in one piece and I probably would not have found the courage or strength to get out of bed, let alone write again.

To all of you strong, funny, talented and great women, I thank you from the bottom of my heart.

Suzan

CONTENTS

DEDICATION iii

CONTENTS iv

INTRODUCTION 1

PROLOGUE 2

One 5

Two 9

Three 12

Four 15

Five 17

Six 18

Seven 21

Eight 25

Nine 28

Ten 32

Eleven 43

Twelve 46

Thirteen 49

Fourteen 51

Fifteen 55

Sixteen 59

Seventeen 63

Eighteen 64

Nineteen 66

Twenty 74

Twenty-One 82

Twenty-Two 85

Twenty-Three 92

Twenty-Four 98

EPILOGUE 101

INTRODUCTION

Saving Moirra's Heart is the continuation of a story that I wrote in 2014, titled *Stealing Moirra's Heart*, originally published in November 2014 as part of *The Highland Winds Collection*. The collection was a collaboration with six other authors, all of whom I adore. Seven novellas, all with their own unique stories that were not connected to one another.

In May, 2015, we released each of those stories as individual novellas. You will need to read *Stealing Moirra's Heart* first in order to better understand this novel. *Stealing Moirra's Heart* is available exclusively at Amazon.

So why publish the continuation now?

I have received countless emails and messages from readers asking for 'the rest of Pillory John and Moirra's story'. I didn't want to wait an entire year before giving it to those who read the first story. While it might have made more sense to wait, to help stave off any confusion, I wanted to get this story in the hands of all those readers who were eagerly awaiting it.

Please feel free to email me at suzan@suzantisdale.com if you have any questions.

PROLOGUE

Alysander woke at dawn with Moirra's bottom snuggled into his groin. 'Twas surely heaven on earth to wake with her in his arms and not have to lie or pretend anymore. Tenderly, with an arm wrapped protectively around her stomach, he pulled her closer, doing his best not to disturb her slumber. Yesterday had been an exhausting one, what with the wolves that had attacked Muriale and Orabilis and the fire that destroyed their little home.

The air in the barn was crisp and smelled of straw and lavender — his wife's favorite scent. He inhaled deeply with the intent to calm his ardor. It was a mistake. Though they had made love twice last night, having her so close to him and knowing he no longer had to hide his feelings for her, well, that just made him want her all the more. As much as he wanted to roll her over and kiss every square inch of her body, he decided to let her sleep. Knowing that they had long days ahead, she would need her rest.

His heart felt much lighter now that their daughters knew the truth. Aye, they were *his* daughters now, no matter what blood might run through their veins and he'd defy anyone to tell him different. His daughters were in the loft, undoubtedly still asleep in the makeshift quarters. Alysander looked forward to rebuilding the cottage and getting everyone out of the barn. On top of having to build a new cottage, they would also need to begin the harvest in a few days.

For the tiniest moment, he thought of reaching out to his father for help, but quickly dismissed the idea. Nay, his father would be of no help to him, for he still blamed the death of his favorite son on his least favorite son, Alysander. He had no doubt the man would let him starve to death before he lifted a finger to help him. He also knew it wouldn't matter one bit that he had turned his life around, had married, and was now the proud father of four beautiful girls.

With a sigh of resignation, he pulled the blankets up around his wife's shoulders, and quietly rolled away. He pulled on tunic and trews, laced up his boots, and stepped away from the bed. He had taken no more than two steps away when he caught sight of Orabilis. The child was curled into a ball on the pallet next to Wulver, with one hand resting on the dog's neck. Aye, she was a stubborn child but he could not blame her for wanting to care for the dog that had saved her life as well as her sister's.

He stepped out of the makeshift bedchamber, found a spare blanket amongst items people had left the night before. Carefully, he draped it over Orabilis and breathed a sigh of relief when Wulver lifted his head and looked at him. He sent a silent prayer up to God before leaving the barn.

Smoke from their destroyed cottage still lingered in the crisp morning air. Morning dew immediately formed on his skin, making him shiver. For now, the fire pit Moirra used to do laundry would have to suffice as a makeshift kitchen. Soon, Alysander had a nice fire going and water heating.

He was able to find a few cooking pots inside the rubble of the burned out cottage. After scouring them thoroughly, they were as good as new. Going through some of the foodstuffs neighbors had thoughtfully brought to them last night, he set about making breakfast for his women. The smell of eggs and sausage frying made its way to the barn and he soon heard the women within shuffling around and readying themselves for the day ahead.

Moirra appeared in the doorway of the barn, looking every bit as beautiful as Aphrodite herself. Her hair was mussed and fell down her back in loose waves. She still looked quite sleepy as she yawned and pulled her shawl around her shoulders. Her eyes searched the yard, and when they fell upon Alysander, a most brilliant smile came to her face. His heart slammed against his chest, his manhood twitched and his mouth went dry. *God's teeth the woman is magnificent.*

"Good morn to ye, husband," she said as she crossed the yard, her smile growing with each step she took.

Alysander swallowed hard as he fought the urge to take her back inside and make love to her again and again.

"Good morn—" his voice caught in his throat. He cleared it and tried again. "Good morn to ye, wife," he said with a smile.

Moirra came to him and wrapped her arms around his waist. "I didna like wakin' up alone," she said against his chest. He placed a gentle kiss on the top of her head and returned her hug.

"But I *did* like wakin' up to the smell of eggs and sausage," she said as she pulled away. Looking into his eyes, she continued to smile. God above, he would never tire of looking at that smile.

"I do believe I told ye once that I know how to cook," he reminded her.

"Aye, and ye do yer own laundry as well," she said playfully. "A man who cooks and cleans without complaint makes me heart go all aflutter. And it makes me want to take ye back to our wee bedchamber and have my way with ye."

He swallowed again and was about to tell her she could do that anytime she wished when the sound of approaching horses drew his attention away.

Instinct warned 'twasn't a social call that brought the five mounted men into Moirra's yard. The two whoresons who had tried to attack Mariote, along with three men Alysander had never seen before, came bounding down the small incline and pulled their horses to a stop.

Alysander heard Moirra's gasp as she stood behind him. It was quickly followed by a flurry of activity inside the barn. Alysander could only assume the girls were either taking up arms or were planning to hide. Knowing him as they did, he imagined it was the former.

A thin man, very much resembling a weasel with unusually large ears, brought his horse to within a few feet of Moirra's door. His gray brown beard hung to the middle of his chest, while his hair was cut very close to his scalp. A hawkish nose sat between a pair of beady eyes. The hair on Alysander's nape stood up. Instantly, he did not like the man who stared down at him as if he were some disgusting creature.

"I see ye hidin', Moirra Wilgart," the man said, looking and sounding perturbed.

Moirra huffed and came to stand beside Alysander. "Me name is Moirra McCullum."

The man huffed derisively and shook his head. "Be this yer latest victim?" he asked, referring to Alysander.

Moirra started to give the man a piece of her mind, but Alysander stopped her by placing a hand on her shoulder. "Who *are* ye?"

"I be Moirra's brother-in-law, Almer Wilgart."

"Ye are no' me brother-in-law," Moirra ground out.

"Ye were married to me brother," Almer said through gritted teeth.

"Nay! I was no'. 'Twas a handfastin' and ye ken it as well as anyone else." She looked then to Alysander. "This is the Sheriff of Glenkirby, and aye, he is Delmar Wilgart's brother."

Alysander never took an eye from any of the men. He gave a slight nod as if he understood completely — which he did not — before asking why they were here.

"I've come to arrest Moirra for the murder of me brother, Delmar Wilgart."

ONE

Pushing Moirra behind him, Alysander stood to his full height, jaw clenched. "What the bloody hell do ye mean ye've come to arrest her?" Questions abounded, blended with his anger that anyone would so unjustly accuse his wife of such an atrocity as murder. 'Twas enough to make his head spin.

The sheriff was unmoved by Alysander's display of protection. He gave a nod to his men, who immediately dismounted. "Me brother's body, or what was left of it, was found last eve."

"What evidence do ye have that my wife killed him?" Alysander challenged, as he kept a close watch on the men slowly approaching.

The sheriff grunted his displeasure at having anyone question his authority. "I don't need any bloody evidence. I *ken* she killed him."

Alysander knew he was sorely outnumbered, and being unarmed did not help his situation. Still, that knowledge did nothing to quell the instinct to protect his wife. When the first man reached out to grab Moirra, Alysander's fury erupted. He swung out, his fist landing hard on the man's jaw. He stumbled backward, his eyes wide with stunned surprise.

In the blink of an eye, Alysander was fighting with such ferocity and fury, he was able to land several punches into the faces and stomachs of the other men. But soon, they had overpowered him and wrestled him to the ground. Moirra's daughters stood frozen in fear just inside the barn, looks of horror on their faces. Moirra and the girls screamed when the sheriff's men began to beat Alysander to a bloody mess.

"Stop!" Moirra called out, momentarily frozen in place, so gripped with fear she could not move. "Stop! Yer killin' him!"

The girls raced from the barn, anger alight in their eyes, *sgian dubh's* drawn and at the ready.

"Nay!" Moirra screamed at her daughters. "Nay!"

Mariote and her sisters came to an abrupt halt, just steps away from the pile of men. Orabilis apparently hadn't heard the order to yield, for she stepped forward and kicked one of the men, her boot landing against his ear. Esa wrapped both arms around her littlest sister and pulled her away.

"Almer!" Moirra shouted as she lunged toward the men, pounding their backs with her fists. "Make them stop!"

One of the men rolled Moirra off with a shrug of his shoulders. She lay on her back, covered in sweat and out of breath. Her daughters rushed to her aid, kneeling beside her. Moirra continued to beg for mercy on Alysander's behalf, tears streaming down her face.

When her words went unheeded, she looked up to Almer. "I'll go with ye!" She screamed. "Just tell them to stop!"

A triumphant and arrogant smile formed on Almer's face before he called his men to stop. "That be enough," he shouted.

The men stood, faces and tunics covered in blood, much of it belonging to Alysander, but some of it their own. Moirra knelt down to look at her husband. His lips were cut and bleeding: both eyes were beginning to swell shut: and bruises covered his face. "Alysander!" she whispered.

He tried to sit but couldn't. His ribs hurt with each breath he took. "Moirra," he said as he reached for her hand.

Two men grabbed her by the arms and pulled her to her feet.

"Moirra," Alysander called out to her. "Moirra!"

The last thing he saw before blackness enveloped him, were the tears streaming down Moirra's face as the sheriff and his men hauled her away.

Moirra's daughters begged and pleaded for her not to go. They pulled at her skirts, chasing the sheriff and his men down the road. Orabilis let loose a slew of curses that would have made Alysander quite proud were he not currently unconscious. Without horses or weapons there was very little they could do for their mum.

Grief stricken, they returned to Alysander, falling to their knees beside him. Mariote gave him a quick assessment and immediately took charge of the situation.

"Esa, fetch water and bandages," Mariote told her as she lifted Alysander's head into her lap. "Muriale and Orabilis, bring blankets and a pillow."

Alysander groaned as he struggled to sit. "Wheest, Da," Mariote whispered. "Do no' try to move yet."

Had Alysander not felt as though he'd been kicked repeatedly in the chest by an angry stallion, he may have taken some delight in hearing Mariote call him *Da*. He was in far too much pain at that moment for much of anything to make sense.

He floated in and out of awareness, having the vague sense that he was being drug into the barn and rolled into the bed he shared with Moirra.

Moirra.

He had to help her, had to get her away from the sheriff. *Why on earth had they accused her of murder?* Was this Almer Wilgart fellow so filled with hatred and deceit that he'd accuse an innocent woman? There was no time to figure it all out now. He had to get to his wife.

Soon, Mariote was washing away blood from his face and hands. Muriale carefully covered him with a blanket and sat down on the ground beside him.

"What do we do now?" Esa asked no one in particular.

Mariote had few answers at the moment. Her first priority was to tend to Alysander's wounds. After that task was completed, she could focus on how to get her mother back.

"How did they find his body?" Muriale asked, looking to her oldest sister for answers.

Mariote went pale before she shushed her sister.

Muriale rolled her eyes in frustration. "We need to tell Alysander the truth. There be no hidin' it now."

Alysander mumbled incoherently as he struggled to sit. "Alysander," Mariote whispered soothingly, "please, I beg ye to no' move yet."

He cursed under his breath right before his head fell back against the pillow.

"I say we get swords and kill the sheriff," Orabilis offered. "If we had swords, we could get mum back."

Her sisters sighed and shook their heads at their naive six-year-old sister. "Orabilis," Esa said as she patted the child on her head, "the four of us can no' go up against the sheriff and all his men."

Orabilis drew her brows inward, looking quite disappointed in her sisters. "I hate the sheriff and his men."

This drew no argument from her sisters.

Mariote finished washing Alysander's cuts and scrapes as best she could. "We need Deirdre," she said as she looked up at Muriale. "I do no' ken how badly he's hurt."

Muriale gave a nod and pushed herself to her feet. "Esa, come with me," she said as she headed toward the one occupied stall.

"Where are ye goin'?" Orabilis asked.

"To saddle Alysander's horse. 'Twill be faster to ride to Deirdre's than to walk."

It took some effort, but eventually, Muriale and Esa had the highland pony saddled and were on their way.

"What do we do now?" Orabilis asked as she and Mariote sat on little stools and stared at the large man before them.

Mariote wanted to scream that she didn't know. Just because she was the oldest did not mean she had the answers to all the world's problems. She felt quite lost at the moment. Though she was certain Alysander would survive the beating he'd suffered at the hands of Almer Wilgart's men, she was not certain her mother would survive whatever hell the sheriff was sure to put her through. Her heart ached with the realization that this was all her own fault.

Tears stung her eyes. Turning away to hide her shame, she swiped at her cheeks. Orabilis was soon beside her, wrapping her little arms around Mariote's shoulders. "Mum will be well," the little girl said softly. "Ye'll see, Mariote."

Mariote knew her sister meant well. Deep down however, Mariote knew that when it was all said and done, none of them would ever be *well* again.

TWO

Not more than an hour passed before Alysander began to regain his senses. He woke with a start, bolted upright in the bed and instantly regretted doing so. His head swam, his face ached, and his tongue felt as though it were made of wool.

Mariote offered him a tankard of cool cider, which he drank greedily.

"What the bloody hell happened?" Alysander asked as he tried to shake the cobwebs from his mind.

Mariote quickly recounted the events of the morning. Tears dripped from her chin as she explained .

Alysander's memory began to return as Mariote spoke. Along with the memories came rage. "Why on earth does the sheriff think yer mum killed Delmar?" Alysander asked, his head spinning.

Mariote chewed her bottom lip as she glanced at her little sister, who was sitting on the floor next to her dog.

Alysander immediately picked up on Mariote's reluctance. He took a deep breath, placed his palms on his knees and forced himself to stand. Mariote was beside him instantly, draping an arm around his waist to keep him from falling. "Ye need to rest," she chastised him.

"Nay," Alysander ground out. "I need answers."

Mariote let loose a frustrated breath.

"Orabilis," Alysander said, "stay with yer pup. I need yer sister's help." Without waiting for an answer or comment from either girl, with Mariote's assistance, Alysander made his way out of the barn and toward the cottage.

Standing near the remnants of their burned out cottage, Alysander let go of Mariote and leaned against one of the remaining stone walls. "I will ask ye again why the sheriff thinks yer mum killed Delmar," Alysander spoke with a calmness that belied how he truly felt. "And I'll have nothin' but the truth, Mariote."

Mariote chewed on her lip again, twisting her fingers together nervously. "Mum didna kill him," she said.

Alysander believed she told the truth, but his gut warned that there was much more Mariote needed to tell him. The pounding in his head increased, but he pushed the pain aside and waited patiently for the girl to continue. When she was silent for too long, he sighed in frustration. "Mariote," he said impatiently, "do no' tarry! I need the truth, lass, and I need it now, or else I'll no' be able to help yer mum."

'Twas a secret that had plagued her for months now, one that ate at her from the inside out. She could no longer hold it in. Tears streamed down her cheeks and trailed their way down her neck. "Mum didna kill Delmar," she repeated. The words were lodged in her throat, and she felt if she didn't get them out, they'd strangle her.

Sobbing and feeling quite sick to her stomach, she choked the words free. "Muriale did."

Muriale? Muriale killed Delmar? Alysander could not believe what he had just heard.

It all came pouring out of Mariote then, in a flood of tears and torment. "'Twas last winter. Orabilis was ill and mum was taking care of her. She was so verra sick and we didna think she would survive much longer. Her fevers were ragin' something fierce. I went to the barn to feed the cow and to pray." Mariote wiped her tears on the sleeve of her dress and took a deep breath before speaking again.

"I did no' like Delmar. I couldna quite say *why* I did no' like him, but there was somethin' about the man I did no' trust. He was always lookin' at me oddly." Mariote cleared her throat and took another deep breath. "I did no' hear him come up behind me. One moment I'm feedin' the cow, the next thing I ken, he's got his hand over my mouth and he's pulling me into the stall. I tried to fight him, I did! I kicked and scratched and bit, but it only angered him. He slapped me so hard across me face that I lost a tooth!"

Mariote shuddered at the memory. The overwhelming sense of helplessness she felt that night washed over her again, and 'twas all she could do not to fall to the ground in a crying heap. "He was goin' to rape me. I could no' move, could no' scream; he had me pinned. The next thing I knew, Muriale was there, plungin' her *sgian dubh* into his back again and again and again! There was blood everywhere."

Mariote's shoulders shook as she sobbed. "He was dead. Muriale killed him because he was tryin' to rape me."

Alysander stood momentarily dumbfounded. The agony etched on Mariote's face, the tears that fell like the harshest highland rains, made his heart feel tight in his chest. He went to her as best he could, and wrapped an arm around her. She fell against his chest, sobbing uncontrollably.

"Wheesht, lass, wheesht," he whispered.

His mind was a whirlwind, racing from one thought to the next. *How could sweet, tiny Muriale kill a man?* Alysander reckoned that even the smallest of individuals could find the strength necessary to complete acts of untold bravery when necessary. He was torn between feeling both shocked and proud of the eleven-year-old girl.

"I must get to Glenkirby," Alysander told Mariote. "But I do no' want to leave ye and yer sisters alone."

Mariote took a deep breath and shuddered. "Ye do no' hate us?" she asked, her voice barely above a whisper.

"Nay!" Alysander exclaimed. "Ye all did what ye must to protect one another. I can no' blame ye for that, Mariote."

Her shoulders sagged with relief. Alysander could take no more of her suffering. "Mariote, do no' fret over it anymore. Ye've suffered enough these past months. The way I see it, Delmar Wilgart got exactly what he deserved."

Mariote sobbed into his chest. "But now mum has been arrested, and she did nothin' wrong!"

Alysander took in a deep breath that nearly knocked him off his feet. His ribs ached with a ferocity he wouldn't have thought possible. But his physical pain was of no import at the moment. "Aye, that is true. But I swear to ye, I'll do whatever I must to free her. I swear it."

"Does that mean we can kill the sheriff and his men?" A small voice spoke from behind them. 'Twas Orabilis.

Alysander turned to look at the wee child, amazed her apparent lust for blood and vengeance. "Nay, it does no'," he told her.

The child shook her head in disgust, placed her hands on her hips and huffed. "I thought ye were brave, Alysander," she challenged him.

He could not resist the smile that accompanied her words. "I am brave, lass. But it does no' mean we can just go killin' people. This day, we must choose the right and just path and free yer mum *legally*."

Orabilis shook her head again. "And if that path leads nowhere?"

Damn, she is every bit her mother's child! Alysander thought. "Then and *only* then will we take up arms." He did not truly believe it would come to that, but he wanted to appease the child.

"Verra well then," Orabilis said, looking satisfied with his answer. "What do we do *now?*"

Unfortunately, Alysander had no immediate answer.

THREE

Almer and his men made their way through the streets of Glenkirby. Moirra did her best to keep her head held high and ignored the people staring her. Word had spread quickly, and by the time they reached the sheriff's office, a sizable crowd had formed.

The onlookers stared unabashedly at Moirra as Wilgart practically tossed her to the ground. Had she not been paying attention, she would have landed on her bottom in the mud.

Within moments, she'd been rushed inside the small, dark building. Almer still refused to tell her anything about the charges lodged against her. She had tried repeatedly to get him to divulge some information on their way to Glenkirby, but he'd refused.

Three steps led down into a small room. A small table and chair sat to the left, while a larger table and two chairs took up most of the wall ahead of her. To her right was a large wooden door that led to the cells. The scent of mold and sweat assaulted her senses.

"Put her in the cell at the back," Almer said as he removed his sword from his belt and laid it on the large table. "The less I see or hear her, the better."

Moirra wasn't about to be led away without an explanation. Digging her heels in, she refused to take another step forward. "I demand to know *why* ye've arrested me, Almer!"

"I told ye before, ye daft woman, ye've been arrested for murder!" Almer yelled at her from across the room.

Moirra lifted her chin defiantly. "What evidence do ye have that Delmar's been murdered? And what evidence that *I* murdered him?"

Almer's face turned red with fury. He slammed his hand down on the table before him. The sound made Moirra jump. "My brother's dead body — or what was left of it after the wolves feasted on it — is *all* the evidence I need!"

Moirra had never liked Almer Wilgart. Today, she loathed him. But seeing his barely controlled anger made her begin to fear him.

Almer gave a dismissive wave of his hand and a moment later, his men took her away.

Moirra's stomach turned when she was tossed into the small, filthy cell. Rotten, urine soaked rushes littered the cold stone floor. A small cot sat against the wall to her right. There was nothing else in the bare space, not even a blanket or chamber pot. Hope dwindled.

A sliver of light shone through the small, narrow window near the top of the damp, lichen covered wall. Even if she stood on the cot, she'd not be able to reach the window. And if she could have reached it, the heavy bars would prohibit any kind of escape.

Thick, black bars separated her cell from the empty one beside it. If she was correct in her estimation, her cell butted against an alley. The only thing she could hear was the faint sound of water dripping outside and something scurrying around in the darkness.

She had no desire to learn what kind of tiny creatures inhabited the dingy mattress on the cot. Pacing around the cramped space only stirred up fetid rushes and made the place smell even worse. Lifting her skirts, she used her booted feet to shove the nasty rushes into a pile near the door. It was all she could do not to wretch, so she covered her nose with the sleeve of her dress.

'Twasn't so much a desire for cleanliness that made her clear a path. Nay, in truth, she was doing whatever she could to keep her mind from worry. But as soon as she was finished, she had nothing left to distract her.

Her heart felt heavy with worry over Alysander and her daughters. He had been unconscious when she was hauled away, his face bloody, his body lying limp on the cold ground. She could only pray that his injuries looked worse than they were. Her only comforting thought was knowing Mariote could tend to his wounds or send word to Deirdre, asking for help.

Moirra refused to release the tears that were welling in her eyes. Leaning against the gritty stone walls, she closed her eyes and buried her face in the crook of her arm. What would become of her daughters? Would Alysander stay and raise them? Would he keep them from doing something stupid, such as coming to the sheriff and telling him the truth?

It was doubtful Almer would believe anything they told him. For whatever reason, he hated Moirra vehemently, and she could never reason out why. Since the day Delmar informed him of their handfasting, his brother had shown nothing but hatred toward Moirra. And now? Now he would see her hang.

Even if her daughters confessed, Moirra knew she would be the one to hang for his murder. It mattered not to Almer what the truth might be, only that Moirra would suffer.

FOUR

'Twas near time for the noonin' meal when Muriale and Esa returned with Deirdre and James McGregor. In the basket Deirdre carried were herbs, poultices, clean bandages, a jar of leeches and various other items she used for healing. Her older brother James was armed to the teeth with broadsword, daggers, and quiver and bow. If Almer Wilgart decided to return, James did not want to be caught unarmed.

Alysander was sick with worry over his wife, wanting nothing more than to head to Glenkirby and demand her release. But without his mount and in his current state, walking there would have been futile.

As soon as the group bounded into the small yard, Alysander raced out of the barn and headed directly toward his horse. "Down with ye," he said as he began helping Muriale and Esa dismount.

"Lord above," Deirdre whispered as she slid from her horse and went to Alysander. "How can ye even see?"

Alysander grabbed the reins and turned to look at Deirdre. "I need ye to take me daughters to yer home," he said. "I am going to Glenkirby."

Deirdre placed a hand on his arm to stop him. "Nay, I do no' think that is such a good idea. Ye've been injured—"

Alysander cut her off. "I've had the bloody hell beaten out of me, but that does no' matter at the moment!" he barked, yanking his arm away from her. "Me wife has been taken by the sheriff, accused of a murder she did *no'* commit. I must help her!"

Deirdre cast him a stern look. "And ye will no' be able to help her if yer dead. Let me tend to yer injuries first.

"Let Deirdre treat ye," James told him. "Then I will help ye think of a way to get Moirra out of there."

When he saw the worried faces of his daughters, Alysander let loose a frustrated breath. He supposed Deirdre was right, in that he would probably pass out before he made it halfway to Glenkirby. Annoyed, he handed the reins off to James and nodded to Deirdre. "Verra well. I shall let ye tend to me, but I beg ye no' to tarry. Moirra needs me."

FIVE

The days crawled by at an agonizingly slow pace. Alysander and the girls were working very hard to rebuild the little cottage. They wanted it put back to rights for the time Moirra would be set free and could return home to them. Alysander tried to absorb some of his stepdaughters' optimism. However, he was having a difficult time convincing himself that all would be well. James had left for Stirling three days ago. Lord willing, he would be there in a few days. Lord willing, he would be able to get the missive to Finnis. Lord willing.

Long conversations took place between Alysander, Mariote and Muriale. The girls believed if they simply went to Almer and confessed the truth, that Muriale had killed Delmar in defense of her sister, then the man would have to let Moirra go free. Alysander knew better.

"Lasses, I ken ye want only to help yer mum, and I could no' be more proud of ye," he told them one night as they sat around the fire. "But ye do no' understand the likes of Almer Wilgart. He cares nothing for justice or truth."

Mariote sighed heavily as she stirred the rabbit stew she was preparing for their supper. "I understand him well enough, Alysander. He's an arrogant man, that I'll give ye. But can ye no' agree that even an arrogant man will see the truth if 'tis laid before him?"

"An arrogant man might," Alysander said. *But an evil and arrogant man?* He added silently.

At dawn each day, Alysander had ridden into Glenkirby to petition for a meeting with his wife. He was denied each and every time. It was slowly killing him inside not knowing how Moirra was doing.

SIX

"I demand ye release me wife, *now*," Alysander said through gritted teeth.

The sheriff sat behind the table, looking up with an arrogant smile that Alysander wished he could wipe from his face. "Nay," Almer said flatly. "I do no' think ye be in any position to demand anythin'. Moirra has been duly charged. She'll stay where she is until she hangs."

It took every bit of energy Alysander owned to keep his temper in check and not unsheathe his sword and run it through the man's heart. He took in one slow, deep breath before responding. "She's been charged, but has no' yet received a trial. How can ye hang someone without a proper trial?"

Almer cocked a brow and leaned back in his chair. "In addition to bein' a thief, ye also be a man of law, aye?"

"I'm neither thief nor solicitor, Almer, nor a fool. I ken ye can't hang a person without a trial," Alysander said.

Almer found great amusement in the statement. He chuckled before rising to his feet. "Verra well then, if 'tis a trial ye want, 'tis a trial we shall have."

Alysander watched the weaselly man carefully with his hand resting on the hilt of his sword. He did not trust him in the least.

"We'll have the trial *now*," Almer announced with a wave of his hand to one of his men as he smiled triumphantly.

Alysander shook his head and crossed his arms over his chest. "Nay," he said calmly.

Almer feigned surprise. "Nay? But ye be right. I canna hang her without a trial. So we'll have the trial now, as ye've demanded. She'll be found guilty and I can hang the stupid wench at dawn on the morrow."

"Do ye truly think me that big a fool?" Alysander asked, his voice calm, his insides anything but.

Almer chuckled again, confident he was in complete control of the situation. "Aye," he said. "A fool. A fool for gettin' yerslef involved with Moirra Wilgart."

Alysander gave a slow shake of his head. "Moirra McCullum."

"Whatever it is ye choose to call the woman, it matters no' to me. She'll hang on the morrow just the same."

"I think no'," Alysander said with another slow shake of his head.

"What makes ye so confident?" Almer asked with a tilt of his head.

'Twas Alysander's turn to smile confidently. "Because I've petitioned Robert."

Almer's brow drew into a line of confusion. "Robert? Robert who?"

"The only Robert that matters. *The* Robert. Robert II, Guardian of Scotland." Robert II held that position whilst David had been—and still was—prisoner to the English these past eight years.

Realization dawned slowly. Almer's arrogant smile was replaced with a look of stunned surprise before his face turned red with anger. "Ye jest?"

"Nay." Alysander took a step forward. "I do no' jest. King David is me cousin, ye see." That was mostly true. A very distant cousin on his mother's side. Alysander had never personally met the man, but Almer needn't know that. Alysander could only hope it would be enough to persuade the sheriff to allow Moirra to go free until a true and proper trial could be set.

Almer's lips thinned as his breathing increased. "Do ye truly expect me to believe ye be a cousin to David, the King of Scotland?"

Alysander shrugged his shoulders. "It matters no' to me what ye believe. Ye can ask Robert's emissary when he arrives."

Almer balled his hands into fists. "Robert's emissary?" he asked, shaking his head in disbelief. "Now ye want me to believe Robert II is sending an emissary?"

'Twas true that Alysander had petitioned Robert. But he had also sent word to Finnis Malcolm, who happened to be one of David's emissaries currently working for Robert II. Alysander had known Finnis more than twenty years, since they were lads too young to shave. The only man he could put any hope in at the moment was Finnis. "Again, I do no' care what ye do or do no' believe. But I can tell ye this," he leaned in, placing his hands on the top of the table. "If anythin' happens to me wife, anythin' at all, before David's emissary arrives, *ye* and ye alone, *will* be held responsible."

"Are ye threatening me?" Almer asked with a look of revulsion.

Alysander stood upright. "Nay, 'tis no threat, Almer. It be a promise."

Alysander all but held his breath as he waited for Almer to think about the implications. While the sheriff may have been as dumb as a basket of rocks, he was not so much a fool as to take a chance by angering the King of Scotland or Robert II. He looked mad enough to bite his sword in half.

Backed into a corner as he was, he had very little choice in the matter. "Verra well," he said as he pushed away from his desk. "The trial will be set for thirty days from now."

'Twas all Alysander could do to keep from shouting with joy. Biting his tongue, he stood taller and did his best not to look overcome with relief.

"But I swear to ye, McCullum, if yer emissary does no' arrive, I will have the trial without him, and Moirra will hang. And if I find ye lied about being the king's cousin, ye'll hang beside her."

There were so many things Alysander wanted to tell the repugnant man, but he knew 'twould be best to hold his tongue for now. He'd just received a thirty-day reprieve. Insulting the man now could only lead to his wife's death, and perhaps his own. "I have no doubt that David's emissary is on his way to Glenkirby as we speak."

Hopefully, he wouldn't stop at every brothel or tavern along the way.

SEVEN

Deirdre McGregor knew Almer Wilgart very well. She'd known him since she was a little girl, for he was one of her brother, Thomas's, best friends. 'Twas a friendship she could never quite figure out, for the two men were as different as night and day. They had nothing in common save for their strong dislike of Moirra. She supposed Thomas hated Moirra because she had repeatedly turned down his proposals. Almer hated her simply because Thomas was his only true friend, and if Thomas hated her, then Almer believed he should. Moirra was a kind, generous woman and Deirdre's closest friend.

Swallowing her pride, Deirdre decided to use the friendship between her brother and Almer to her advantage. Standing before the sheriff, she pushed her shoulders back and offered him her most sincere smile. She nearly choked on the sweet words she voiced to the man.

"So ye see, Almer, I want only to make certain that Moirra is healthy and well. I would hate for the King's Emissary to think ye didna take good care of her."

She knew full well Almer was not taking any kind of care of Moirra. It wasn't in his nature to show kindness to anyone, least of all someone he hated. Still, she had to stroke his ego if she were to have any chance at seeing her friend.

Almer gave the matter some thought before finally agreeing. "Verra well, Deirdre. I shall let ye see the prisoner, but only fer a short time."

Smiling as sweetly as she could, she thanked him for his kindness. What she frankly wished she could do was run a dirk through his ugly, dark heart.

Deirdre was unable to quash the gasp of shock that came upon seeing Moirra for the first time in days. Gaunt and pale, dark circles had formed under the woman's eyes. Deirdre rushed into the cell, the smell of urine, vomit and feces assaulting her senses as she knelt before her dearest friend.

"Deirdre," Moirra whispered, sounding dazed and confused.

"Moirra, what have they done to ye?" Deirdre took Moirra's hands in hers. They felt as cold as ice. Looking into Moirra's eyes, she saw they were glassy and vacant. The woman staring back at her was not the same Moirra who Deirdre had called friend for all these many years.

Locked in the God-forsaken space for nearly a week, enduring heaven only knew what, had taken the spark from Moirra's eyes.

"I want to go home, Deirdre," Moirra whispered. "I want to see me girls and Alysander."

Deirdre began to rub warmth into her friend's hands. "I ken ye do, Moirra. I swear, we be doin' our best to get ye home. Please, do no' give up hope."

Moirra blinked a few times before she found her voice again. "Hope?" she sighed. "I'm afraid I lost all hope days ago. I'm cold, filthy, tired, and hungry. They give me nothin' but bread and bad water. I canna keep anything down, Deirdre. It all comes back up."

Deirdre felt quite certain that under these circumstances she wouldn't be able to keep any food in her stomach either. "Wheesht, now," she said as she removed her cloak and draped it around Moirra. "To keep yer spirits up, why do ye no' try to imagine Almer's soul burnin' in hell? Or better yet, imagine all the different ways yer husband might kill him." Her attempt at levity was meant to bolster Moirra's spirits. It had the opposite affect.

Tears began to fall down her cheeks, as her face twisted with pain and heartache. "I fear he does no' care fer me any longer," she wept.

Deirdre was stunned at the accusation. "Are ye daft? The man does no' sleep, he barely eats. He is sick with worry over ye."

Moirra looked puzzled as she wiped tears from her cheeks with the cloak. "Why has he no' come to see me?"

Deirdre let out a frustrated sigh. If she ever had the opportunity to kill Almer Wilgart, she'd take it. "Alysander has been here every day. He begs to see ye, but Almer will no' let him."

Moirra blinked, her brow scrunched in undeniable confusion. "But they said Alysander has yet to show his face here."

"Remember who we be dealin' with. Almer? George? Harry? They all be bloody cruel men. They lie to keep ye depressed and hurtin'."

A glimmer of the strong, independent Moirra began to flicker back to life. "Why would they do that? Why will they no' let me see him?"

Deirdre shook her head. "If we could figure that out, we could solve many of the world's problems. Ye ken that as well as me, Moirra. They take great pleasure in hurtin' people."

Moirra sniffled and wiped away the last of her tears. "Why do they hate me so?"

Deirdre smiled warmly. "Ye keep askin' me things I canna answer. Try askin' somethin' I *can*."

"How be me girls? How is Alysander?"

"They be well, though they do miss ye somethin' fierce. Little Orabilis made a call to arms and says we should just come and get ye, and if Almer gets in their way, well too bad fer him."

For the first time in days, Moirra giggled. "Is she still askin' fer her own broadsword?"

"Aye, and I fear she'll wear Alysander down to the point he'll give her one," Deirdre replied.

Deirdre was tempted to scream, remove the *sgian dubh* from her belt and seek out Almer right then. Instead, she removed a bladder of water from her basket and washed Moirra's face as best she could. Once she was done, she left the disgusting cell to speak with the sheriff.

Still at his desk, with his dirty booted feet propped up on it, he and George were discussing something, but stopped when Deirdre entered the room. She walked straight to him, set her basket at her feet, and looked him in the eye. "If ye do no' give Moirra a clean cell *now*, I will no' only write to the king, I shall let his emissary ken how ill ye've taken care of her. If ye do no' see to it that she has clean blankets, a clean chamber pot, and something more than bread to eat, I will tell me brothers James, William and Phillip that ye made improper advances toward me."

Almer shot to his feet, looking as insulted as he was angry. "Ye would no' dare!"

Hands on her hips, she said, "Would ye like to find out?"

Deirdre knew there were very few people on this planet that Almer was afraid of. Four to be exact. James, William and Phillip terrified him the most. He knew, without question, that if Deirdre did as she had promised, he'd not live to see another day. While Thomas did care for her, he would see right through any false accusations. James, William and Phillip, however, would take any opportunity to beat the bloody hell out of Almer and his cohorts, even if they knew there was a chance she was being less than truthful. They took their roles as older, protective brothers quite seriously. They'd defend Deirdre to their own deaths if need be.

Angrily, Almer shouted at George. "Go put Moirra in a clean cell!"

George stood, his expression confused. "We do no' have a clean cell. They all look like hers."

"Then go clean one!" he yelled across the room.

George made a hasty retreat, heading through the door that separated them from the cells.

Deidre called out after him. "And make sure ye lay down clean rushes!"

She turned back to Almer. "I thank ye, kindly, Almer. 'Tis fer yer own good that I make these requests."

With flared nostrils and a purple face, Almer said, "Requests?"

Deirdre resisted the urge to laugh at him. Instead, she feigned innocence. "Please fergive me. As a healer, I want only what is best fer those in me charge. Even ye must admit the conditions here are an abomination. I would no' even let me animals inside one of those cells."

Almer didn't need to say he didn't believe her. His expression said it all. Deirdre didn't truly care.

"I shall be back later today," Deirdre warned him. "With clean clothing for Moirra. I expect ye'll no' argue about that, or anythin' else that will make her time here a bit more bearable."

"Keep in mind, Deirdre, that she be a prisoner, no' a queen or a member of the aristocracy," his voice dripped with venom.

"I ken verra well who she be, Almer. But ye must also remember that she is married to Alysander McCullum. And Alysander is cousin to the king. So by default, she *is* a member of the aristocracy, no matter how much ye do no' wish to admit it."

"I believe *that* as much as I believe yer nothin' but a sweet, innocent lass," he said.

Deirdre took a step toward him. "Then why, praytell, did ye set the trial fer a month away?"

He said nothing, though Deirdre noticed he was clenching and unclenching his fists. It did not worry her in the least, for she knew he would never do anything to her out of fear of angering her brothers.

Grabbing her basket, she told him she would be back in a few hours. "Ye should be glad, Almer, fer my sensibilities. If the king's emissary saw how ye were treatin' Moirra, well, it might be *ye* in that cell instead of her."

EIGHT

Finnis Malcolm had wasted no time in petitioning Robert II to allow him to travel to Glenkirby. Even though his argument was weak at best, the fact that even one of David's distant cousins was sitting in a dank prison, accused of a crime that her husband was convinced she hadn't committed was enough to sway David. Finnis left that very day, with James McGregor and a small envoy of the king's men.

They arrived in Glenkirby just after dawn, ten days after he had received Alysander's request for help. Finnis had not heard from the man in more than a year—not since they had received word of his brother, Hugh's death. He had, however, been in communication with Alysander's older brother, Connor.

Finnis had been wholeheartedly stunned when he received Alysander's letter. He was even more stunned to learn that he had married—a woman with four daughters. Try as he might, Finnis could not envision Alysander as a father of one child, let alone four daughters. 'Twas more than just concern for his friend's well being that sealed his decision to ride to Glenkirby; 'twas the sheer curiosity of needing to find out how Alysander had come by a wife and daughters, and how he was getting along with domesticity.

On their journey to Glenkirby, James had been full of quite useful information, especially as it pertained to Almer Wilgart and the men who worked for him. 'Twas James' fervent belief that Moirra was innocent. If Delmar had been murdered, there was a whole list of suspects to choose from. As far as James was concerned, Moirra was not on that list. There was no need for her to kill the man, for they were in a handfast, not a legally binding marriage. She could leave him at any time, so murdering him for her freedom was out of the question.

James McGregor led Finnis and his men to the Brown Boar Inn, the only inn Glenkirby possessed. As soon as Finnis had procured rooms for he and his men, James took him to meet the sheriff.

To say he was not impressed with the vile weasel of a man, would have been a tremendous understatement. Besides finding the man's body odor more foul than a pigsty, he also found him to be a groveling fool. Finnis seriously doubted the man behaved this way toward anyone else.

"I must confess," Almer said after the appropriate introductions had been made, "I did not believe Alysander McCullum."

"On what matter?" Finnis asked as he removed his gloves and tucked them under his arm. There was a small brazier in a corner of the room. Finnis went to it to warm his hands.

"On any matter," Almer replied. "The man be a thief, a poor one, but a thief all the same. If a man will steal, he will lie."

Almer had no idea that the 'thief' to whom he referred was Finnis's oldest and closest friend. Purposefully, he left that information out of the formal introductions and had asked James to do the same. He was here to act as the judge and overseer of Moirra McCullum's trial. Who knew how anyone would behave should they learn the truth?

"A thief, ye say?" Finnis asked, feigning ignorance. James had filled him in on the events that led to Alysander and Moirra meeting, insomuch as he knew them. Though he doubted Almer Wigert's description of the events would cast Alysander in any kind of favorable light.

"Aye," Almer said as he sat in a wooden chair on the other side of the brazier. "He was caught stealin' a necklace from one of the merchants. The necklace was in his pocket."

Finnis knew Alysander well enough to know that he would never steal anything from anyone. There had to be more to the story, and he was determined to find out.

"Well, now that yer here, we can have the trial this day," Almer said, his eagerness undeniable.

Almer had no good idea yet that attempts to order Finnis to do anything were extremely foolish.

"Nay," Finnis said as he began to stuff his hands into his gloves. "I have just arrived this morn. We have travelled far in a short time."

"On the morrow, then," Almer said with far too much zeal.

Finnis headed toward the door to leave. "I will let ye ken when the trial will begin."

A flicker of annoyance flashed in the sheriff's eyes, but he remained mute.

Finnis left a very annoyed Almer where he stood, without so much as a by-your-leave. He had questions, lots of questions. And Alysander

McCullum was the only one who could answer them.

Because they could not risk being observed publicly, Finnis made arrangements for them to meet in the small thicket of woods near Moirra's land.

'Twas a great relief for Alysander to see his old friend. "Finnis," Alysander said, giving him a manly hug and slap on the back. "I can no' tell ye how glad I am that yer here."

"'Tis curiosity more than anythin' else that brings me," Finnis said as he studied his friend closely. Dark circles had formed under Alysander's eyes; eyes that no matter how big a smile he put on his face, were filled with worry. "When was the last time ye slept?"

Alysander would not insult Finnis by pretending all was right in his world. They'd known each other far too long. "No' since they took Moirra."

Finnis quirked one brow. "She must be somethin' verra special, fer I thought I'd never see the day when ye'd be married."

Alysander smiled weakly and nodded. "Aye, she be verra special Finnis, more special than ye can imagine."

NINE

"Ye have a visitor, Moirra," Harry taunted her through the bars of her cell. "Do ye think it be yer husband? Yer children?"

Moirra sat on the edge of her cot, wishing for all the world that a bolt of lightening would somehow find its way to the top of his ugly head. Between Harry, George and Almer, she was growing quite fed up with their continuous assault of insults and taunts.

"Nay," Harry said. "Ye've shamed them too much, ye ken. They will no' come to see ye, fer yer too big a disappointment to them. Poor things canna even walk down the streets without bein' shunned by everyone."

"Taunt me all ye wish, Harry, I do no' care. When yer here doing that, it means yer no' out trying to molest or rape some young innocent girl," she told him with a casual air.

His smile vanished as he lunged forward. "At least I do no' kill them like yer known to do," he seethed.

Moirra shrugged one shoulder. "I imagine those poor girls wished ye had killed them, fer 'twould be the only way to erase the memory of yer toothless, ugly face and yer foul stench."

"I canna wait to see ye hanged, Moirra. I imagine by this time on the morrow we'll be puttin' the noose around yer neck," he said.

With a roll of her eyes that said she didn't really care what he had to say, she turned away. She was not going to give him or George and Almer the pleasure of seeing her distressed.

George led Moirra's visitor through the heavy wooden door, down the short, narrow hallway and into the large room that housed the cells. With a heavy, dirty boot, Harry kicked a small stool toward Moirra's cell—his way of offering the man a seat.

When Moirra saw who her visitor was, she jumped to her feet and rushed to the bars. "William?" she asked, uncertain why he was there.

"Good day to ye, Moirra," he said as he righted the stool. "I'd ask how ye fare, but me thinks ye'd only lie and tell me yer well." He offered her a warm smile before sitting down.

Quickly, Moirra pulled the tiny cot closer to the bars and sat on the edge. "Why are ye here?" she asked. "Is it me girls? Alysander?" She could not imagine any other reason why he'd be here or why Almer would grant him a visit. Her heart beat rapidly with worry and concern.

"Yer family be just fine, Moirra," he said. "Though we worry that Orabilis will attempt to stage yer rescue at any moment. Alysander has her under constant watch."

Moirra felt much relieved. William's jest over Orabilis almost made her laugh. "Then why are ye here?"

"I have been granted permission to act as yer legal representative," he told her.

Moirra blinked once, then again, quite confused by his proclamation. "Ye?" she asked. "But ye have no experience, do ye?"

William shook his head. "Nay, I fear I do no'."

Moirra studied him for a time. All the McGregor men were blessed with long, blond hair with just enough curl in it to make most women envious. William was no exception. Of all the McGregor brothers, he was by far her favorite. He was kind and had a wicked sense of humor. However, his dark blue eyes were filled with concern at the moment.

"Why ye, though? Do no' mistake me questions as worry, fer I ken ye to be a right smart man," she told him.

He took in a deep breath and let it out in a whoosh. "The truth?" he asked.

Moirra gave a nod. "Aye, William, the truth."

"Yer husband did no' have the funds to pay anyone. I volunteered to help, fer I ken in me heart that ye did no' kill Delmar Wilgart. What misfortune befell the man, I do no' ken. Knowin' him as I did, I believe he probably deserved whatever he got."

Moirra wholeheartedly agreed.

"Moirra, I ken ye did no' kill him. Or if ye did, 'twas more likely an act of self-defense. Either way, I ken that ye do no' possess a vengeful evil bone in yer wee body," he said, his smile returning.

"William, I give ye my word that I did no' kill him," she assured him. *Please, do no' ask me if I ken who did.*

"I believe ye."

They sat quietly for a long moment before William spoke again. "Can ye tell me when ye saw him last?"

When we buried his sorry dead body. "Months ago. I canna remember the exact date, but I do remember that Orabilis was quite ill. I did no' think she would survive."

William thought on it for a moment. "I remember that. 'Twas early last winter, aye?"

"Aye," she said with a nod.

"I took Deirdre to yer home to help ye. I ken Delmar was alive then, because he was complainin' about how Orabilis' cough was disturbin' his sleep."

The truthfulness in his statement made her face burn with shame. How she could have been so stupid to handfast with such a cold-hearted man? "Aye. We argued after ye and Deirdre left." That much was true. "'Twas then that he said he wanted to end the handfast."

William brows arched a bit. "And how did ye feel about that?"

She wasn't about to gloss over it. "I was quite glad fer it and told him so. It saved me the trouble of havin' to call ye and yer brothers back to kick his sorry, lazy arse out of me home."

William chuckled. "I would have come at once, fer I did no' like that man at all."

"Few people did."

"So he left that night?"

"Aye," Moirra answered quietly. "He left that verra night." *He left our wee cottage and went to the barn to try to rape Mariote.*

"Did he take anythin' with him?"

"Aye, though 'twasn't much, ye ken, fer he did no' bring much with him. Just his clothes and a broadsword."

William scratched his jaw while he thought for a short moment. "All those things were found with him," he said. "At least accordin' to Almer. He says the only thing missin' was a bag of coins."

Moirra gave a slight shake of her head. "He did no' have much by the way of coin, William. But I know fer a fact he had it with him when he left." *She had buried it with his body for she did not want anything left of him in her home. Not even the few coins he had.*

"Moirra, can ye think of any one else who would want him dead?" William asked.

When Moirra cast him a look that said she questioned his soundness of mind, William chuckled. "I suppose there were many, aye?"

"Yes, William, there were many who did no' like him and aye, even a few who would want to see him dead."

Orabilis did not like Thomas McGregor, for many reasons. Primarily, however, she detested the way he treated her and her sisters, as well as her pup, Wulver. He refused to allow the sweet-natured dog into his home and had even tried to allow Wulver no refuge anywhere on his lands. But Phillip intervened on her behalf, though in secret, so Thomas wouldn't find out.

Phillip had helped bring Wulver from Orabilis' home to his own. Phillip and his wife were much nicer than Thomas. They even went so far as to make a bed for him, using an old basket, and setting it in front of the hearth in their tiny cottage. Orabilis spent every waking moment sitting beside Wulver, talking to him, helping to change his bandages and applying the salve Deirdre had made for his wounds.

In a matter of days, Wulver was feeling much better. Within a fortnight, he was eating again and was soon up and about and back to his old self. Though Orabilis was quite happy with Wulver's recovery, she still missed her mother something fierce. Her sisters did their best to take care of her, but they were not her mum and that, in turn, caused a good amount of frustration for everyone.

There were only two other people in her world that she hated more than Thomas McGregor; Delmar and Almer Wilgart. Thankfully one of them was already dead.

Her mum and sisters all thought she did not know what had really happened to Delmar. Orabilis decided it best to keep it that way, to continue to pretend she didn't know. If they thought she knew Muriale had actually been the one to kill Delmar, well, they would all worry that she'd not keep it a secret. The last thing anyone of them needed was more worry.

What no one realized was that she was quite good at keeping secrets. She wasn't a tattler like Esa. Nay, Orabilis knew how important it was not to tell anyone what she knew about that night. Her sisters' very lives depended on keeping that secret. What to do about her mother was an altogether different concern. She could not help her mum without tattling on her sisters. And if she did by some chance let it slip that Muriale had killed Delmar and they hanged her for it, well, even at the age of six she knew 'twould be a long time before anyone would forgive her that slip-of-the-tongue.

Nay, no matter what she did or didn't do, someone was in serious trouble. In the end, she supposed it was best to keep the secret *secret* and find another way to help her mum. If only the adults around her would listen and simply put out the call to arms, march in to Glenkirby and remove her mother from gaol, then things could go back to normal.

But adults rarely listened to the good advice of a child.

TEN

After returning to Glenkirby, Finnis went to visit Almer Wilgart. If what James and Alysander had told him was true, then Almer had no real evidence against Moirra. He took with him two of the fifteen men that had ridden with him from Stirling. Alec and Bruce were young men who most people, at first glance, would mistake for idiots, simply because of their size and stature. Nothing could be farther from the truth. A head taller even than Finnis with the appearance of having been built from stone, the men could be counted on for protection as well as intellect.

The sheriff and Finnis sat across from one another at Almer's desk. Almer was just as foul smelling as he had been that morning. Apparently, bathing was not a vital part of the man's life.

Bruce removed the small scroll he had tucked into his belt and handed it to Finnis, who in turn handed it to Almer. "As ye can see from the seal, it be from Robert II, Guardian of Scotland."

Finnis couldn't necessarily describe the expression on Almer's face as one of awe. 'Twas more akin to confusion, surprise, and curiosity. Almer took a small dagger and carefully ran it under the seal. His lips moved as he read each word slowly.

"By his order," Finnis began to explain, "I will act as judge in the proceeding against Moirra Dundotter-McCullum."

Almer began to work his jaw back and forth as he continued to read.

"I ken ye be the sheriff here, Almer Wilgart. But ye also be related to the victim. While the king values yer fealty to him, ye canna act as both sheriff, judge and jury in this matter."

Almer was visibly upset. "Ye believe I canna be fair and just?"

"I do no' believe any man in yer position could be fair and just," Finnis told him. "I ken that I would no' be able to, had it been my brother who was dead."

"I want justice fer me brother," Almer told him with a firm voice.

"As would any man," Finnis agreed. "But we must make certain it be justice that is given, no' vengeance."

Almer angrily tossed the scroll aside. "And if I seek both?"

Finnis arched one brow. "If the woman be truly guilty, ye shall have both. My only concern is for justice. Ye may, of course act as counsel for the crown."

That seemed to ease some of Almer's anger. "Verra well, m'laird. When would ye like the trial to commence?"

"The sooner, the better," Finnis said. Though not for the same reasons Almer wanted to begin. Finnis doubted there was much in the way of evidence but he was still willing to keep an open mind on the matter. "We shall commence on the morrow at ten."

Almer looked pleased with his answer, barely able to contain his excitement.

The more time Finnis spent with the man, the less he liked him. Was Almer as heartless as he was pompous? "Verra well," Finnis said as he stood to leave. "I shall seeyeon the morrow."

At the door, Finnis paused to glance over his shoulder one last time. The sheriff was still smiling. 'Twas a smile that made Finnis's blood run cold.

Finnis was in a most difficult position. As servant to his king and the laws of his country as well an honorable man, he could not allow his friendship with Alysander McCullum to interfere with his duty. It mattered not that he didn't like Almer Wilgart or that he loved Alysander like a brother. The only thing that mattered was the truth.

If the evidence Almer was going to present was strong and proved without any doubt that Moirra had in fact killed Delmar Wilgart, then his only option would be to convict her and sentence her to death. If, however, the evidence was severely lacking, then he would have no qualms in declaring her innocent. If the lines between the two — guilt or innocence — were blurred, his decision would be far more difficult. In the end, it could cost him a friendship. Finnis would always try to err on the side of caution. More than one life was at stake in this situation. If Moirra were hanged, Alysander would die not long after, more likely than not, from a broken heart.

The lives of two people were now in his hands.

He could only pray that he would make the right decision.

Her trial would begin on the morrow. Moirra wasn't sure if she should feel relieved or even more worried.

Almer had informed her that Robert II had sent an emissary to act as overseer of the proceedings. Though he did his best to make her believe it had been at his own request, Moirra didn't fully believe him. Almer was as trustworthy as a wolf left to watch over a flock of sheep. She also seriously doubted he had any connection to the king whatsoever. Had there been any, either he or his brother Delmar would have bragged about it repeatedly.

Tired beyond compare, sleep was elusive. Nay, there had to be more to it than Almer said, but what? Mayhap 'twas all a lie, a ruse to make her feel even more disheartened. Mayhap there was no emissary at all and it was simply another way for the sheriff to torture her.

In the end, the only thing that truly mattered was keeping her daughters safe. If Almer ever learned the truth, he would not give a second thought to hanging Muriale, no matter how young she was. Nay, she would gladly sacrifice her own life so her daughters would have some chance at a future.

If Alysander did not want the responsibility of raising them, Moirra would not hold that against him. Though Deirdre had been quite emphatic that Alysander was sick with worry and had sworn he would raise the girls as his own, Moirra still had lingering doubts. He was a good man, of that there was no doubt. But to take on the task of raising his soon-to-be dead wife's children? That would be a tremendous act of love. One she could carry into eternity with her, that was, if the good Lord saw fit to allow her access.

"Heavenly father," she whispered into the darkness, "on the morrow, they'll make me swear an oath to tell the truth. I be lettin' ye ken now that I'll be lyin' through me teeth." Mayhap if she admitted now that she'd be lying, God would be able to forgive her.

Aye, she was perfectly willing to die to protect her daughters.

The truth was that Delmar Wilgart had been a waste of human flesh. Unfortunately, she hadn't realized it until it was too late. She had only agreed to handfast with him because she needed help with her farm and no one else would have her. Had she realized sooner that Delmar was just as awful as his brother, she would have sold the farm to Thomas McGregor and moved on.

But had she done that, she would not have met Alysander McCullum.

And she would never have been blessed to experience the joy that true love brings. She and Alysander loved one another much like her parents had—without restraint, without condition. Passionately, wholeheartedly. 'Twas a rare kind of love; she had once believed she would never experience it.

But now she had, and it was everything she thought it would be, yet more.

Had she done something in her past that had angered God? 'Twas the only thing that made sense to her at the moment. She'd angered God and this was his way of exacting his vengeance. He'd given her the one thing she had silently longed for the whole of her adult life.

Then He took it all away.

Or was He simply testing her? Testing her faith, strength and resolve?

Either way, she was locked in a cold, dark cell. Punishment for some wrong doing or a test of faith, here she was. Cold, tired, sick with worry and fear. Longing for her husband, her children, wishing she had done so many things differently. Questioning poorly made decisions and wondering how altered her life would be had she not done this or that.

It wasn't the first time Moirra had been with child. But it was the first time she'd found herself locked in a filthy, dank gaol while in this condition. With Deirdre's help, they estimated she was only two months along. The morning sickness was overwhelming, to say the least. She could not remember ever throwing up this much with her four daughters. The excessive vomiting could be, she assumed, due to her horrible living conditions, the worry over her family, and the stress of not knowing when she'd hang. More likely than not, it was all of the above.

If she was found guilty, would they allow her to live long enough to bring Alysander's child into this world? She wondered, if they killed her whilst with child, would anyone besides her consider that murder of an innocent child? 'Twas doubtful that Almer Wilgart would care.

According to the sunlight beaming in through the small window of her cell, morning had dawned bright. Was that another way of God making her suffer? Was this His way of saying *See what ye shall miss, sinner?*

After retching into the bucket, Moirra laid back down on the cot. Though Deirdre had done her best to see that Almer improved the conditions of her cell, it was still a filthy, dark and dank space. Whenever it rained — which was happening more and more frequently this time of year — the water would trickle in through the open window and tiny cracks in the stones. There had been a few times when deep puddles had formed, forcing Moirra to stay to the cot to keep from soaking her feet in the frigid, murky water.

The brazier that sat in the small space outside her cell was lit only once a day and only after nightfall. None of her gaolers bothered to light it again, no matter how cold the night air became.

I treat me cow better than this, she mused as she stared up at the dark ceiling.

Worry and dreadful anticipation draped around her like a wet blanket. Soon, very soon, she'd be led away. But to what end? Her freedom or her death?

Much to her surprise and near glee, George and Harry brought her a bowl of clean water. She washed as best she could and rinsed out her mouth. A while later, they brought her a small hunk of bread, an even smaller hunk of cheese, and a small flagon of cider. Her stomach was too upset to eat anything more than a few bites of bread.

How much time had passed, she neither knew nor cared, but George and Harry did come for her. They led her out of her cell with her hands and feet bound in chains as if she were some great threat.

She recognized most of the faces and knew they were here not to wish her well, but to see her sentenced to death. They didn't care about seeking the truth, of that, she was quite certain.

There had been a time, when she was younger, when the townspeople were kind to her. Her parents had been well respected by all who knew them, and they afforded Moirra the same respect.

But something had begun to change, right around the time she married Kenneth, her first husband. 'Twasn't a sudden change, but something that happened over time. 'Twasn't until the death of her second husband that the townspeople began to openly show their contempt for her. Some would turn and walk the other way when they saw her approach. Others were not so subtle.

'Twas then the rumors—which before had been whispered behind her back—were spoken openly and within earshot. For reasons she could not grasp, the people believed she was responsible for the deaths of her husbands. 'Twas utter nonsense of course, for Kenneth had died of the ague and Aric had been killed in battle. How they thought her responsible for his death remained a mystery.

When she saw Alysander and three of her four daughters sitting in the small chamber, Moirra was tempted to turn and run back to her cell. She did not want them to see her like this: in a dirty dress, her hair unwashed, and bound with shackles at her ankles and wrists.

When Moirra's daughters saw her, they started to jump to their feet and rush to her side. Alysander held them back and whispered something to them that made them return to their seats.

She thought Alysander's smile looked forced and knew he was doing his best to lift her spirits and offer silent hope. Though she didn't feel like smiling, she tried to return his smile all the same. His Adam's apple bobbed once, then twice, as if he were fighting back emotion and tears. When he mouthed the words *I love you,* she nearly fell to her knees with raw heartache. Returning his sentiment was almost impossible without crying, but from somewhere deep within, she found the strength to do it.

What she would not give to be able to wrap her arms around her family once more. Tears she'd been holding on to for days welled in her eyes. She swallowed hard and cleared her throat to keep them at bay. 'Twas bad enough she was dirty and shackled. The last thing they needed to see were her tears.

A hush fell when she was brought to stand in the center of the room. A man she did not recognize sat in a high-backed chair on the dais. He had the look of someone important, what with his regal bearing and fine clothes. Parchments were spread on the table before him, along with a block of wood, ink and quill. He seemed far too young to be an overseer of any trial, let alone hers.

After George and Harry positioned her in the middle of the room, facing the overseer, they stepped away, but not far. The watched over her as if she were a constant threat to the innocent people in the room.

The overseer picked up the block of wood and banged it against the table. Moirra had been watching her family and was caught off guard. The loud bang gave her a start.

"I be Finnis Malcolm, Emissary to Robert II, Guardian of Scotland and King David. I will be actin' as overseer for the trial against Moirra Dundotter-McCullum. Actin' as counsel for the defendant will be William McGregor. Acting on behalf of the crown will be Almer Wilgart."

Moirra didn't know which was worse: Almer acting as her judge or as her prosecutor.

Alysander knew there was no real evidence against his wife. Almer had kept whatever evidence he had against Moirra a secret. There had been no way for William to prepare any kind of defense. He was hopeful that whatever evidence the sheriff might have, it would be so weak as to be laughable. Still, he worried.

He also knew that the sheriff did not necessary *need* any cold, hard evidence or facts in order to convict Moirra in the eyes of the public. All that was required was an accusation. The townspeople would do the rest. Had Finnis Malcolm not been here to oversee the proceedings, Alysander knew his wife would already have been hanged. And the townspeople would have welcomed it.

Even if she were found innocent, her future here was questionable at best. All Almer need do was *accuse* Moirra of a crime. The good people of Glenkirby would, in the end, do his dirty work for him. After all, the good sheriff would not accuse an innocent person, would he? The truth was of little consequence.

But Alysander *did* know the truth. Moirra's only misdeed had been to trust Delmar Wilgart. Trusting the man had been a mistake. Now, it appeared she would have to pay for that mistake with her life.

Alysander glanced at his three step-daughters, who sat next to him on the long bench. Tears streamed down Mariote's face, Esa's lips were drawn into a thin hard line, and Muriale looked ready to take the sheriff's life. Knowing Orabilis was all too keen on war, they had left her with Phillip McGregor and his wife—if not for her own safety then for the safety of those around her.

Oh, how he wished he had had the funds to hire someone from Edinburgh or Stirling to act as legal counsel for his wife! Instead, all he had at the moment was William McGregor. Although Alysander did like the man, there was still the question of where William's fealty lay: with his brother, Thomas, and the sheriff, or with justice? Only time would tell.

The crown, or in this case, Almer Wilgart, would be the first to speak and to question Moirra. He stood off to one side so he could see her as well as the crowded benches filled with onlookers eager to watch as a woman's life hung in the balance.

"Nearly three weeks ago, the body of Delmar Wilgart was found. Or what was left of it," he spoke loudly, attempting to appear as though he knew what he was doing. "Lyin' in a grassy field, with bugs and scavengers feastin' upon him as if he were a rack of lamb."

The mental image he painted made Moirra feel sick to her stomach. The hatred and vehemence she saw on the faces of the onlookers when she chanced a furtive glance toward them, chilled her to the bone. She knew a few of them and found it baffling that those people who Delmar had cheated or bullied over the years, now appeared to mourn his loss. It hit her then, as jarring as being tossed into a frozen loch: they hated her more than they hated Delmar.

Almer continued to drone on about what a good man Delmar had been. If one were to believe him, Delmar should be sainted and Moirra burn at the stake.

"I find it more than a bit odd that all of Moirra Dundotter's husbands are dead," Almer said, shaking his head as if the facts saddened him.

William McGregor stood and asked, "Are ye blamin' Moirra fer the deaths of her first two husbands?"

Almer turned to face him with a hateful glare. "Do ye no' find it suspicious that a woman has three dead husbands?"

William chuckled. "Was no' yer own mum married four times?"

"Shut yer mouth, William! Me mum is no' on trial here!" Almer shouted.

William raised a curious brow. "'Tis a good thing we do no' put anyone on trial fer bein' married more than once, elst the cemetery would be bigger than the village."

The onlookers laughed at that, but it only made Almer angrier.

Finnis knocked the block of wood against his table three times to bring some order to the room. To William, he said, "Sir, ye'll get yer chance to speak soon enough." He then turned his attention to Almer. "How did Moirra's first two husbands die?"

Almer stammered his reply. "What does it matter?"

"It matters because *ye* brought it up, Almer. Ye said ye found it odd that all of her husbands be dead, which leads me to believe ye think she killed them as well." He did not wait for a response. Instead, he looked at Moirra. "Lass, how did yer first two husbands die?"

Moirra swallowed hard before answering. "Me first died of the ague, as did a dozen others in Glenkirby. Me second died in battle against the English, in '51, at Glen Ross."

"Were *ye* at the battle of Glen Ross?" Finnis asked.

The crowd laughed aloud at the question.

"Nay, m'laird, I was no'. I was at home birthin' his child, me youngest daughter, Orabilis."

She could hear soft murmurs coming from the onlookers, but could not understand any of those hushed whispers.

Finnis rested an index finger against his temple. "Almer, do ye still think she killed her first two husbands?"

"Mayhap nay, but I still believe she murdered me brother, and I intend to prove it." His tone was unyielding.

Undeterred, Almer turned his attention back to Moirra. The man was fully determined to prove to the world that Moirra had killed his brother.

"Did ye no' tell me that ye and Delmar had decided to end yer handfastin' early?" Almer asked as he stood between Moirra and Finnis.

Moirra gave a solemn nod. "Aye, I did," she answered. "I also told ye 'twas a mutual agreement."

Almer asked his next question before she even had time to fully answer the last. "And did ye no' also tell me that Delmar said he was goin' to Inverness?"

Moirra swallowed hard before answering. "Aye, I did."

Almer looked quite pleased with her answer and even managed to smile down at her. "Where is Inverness, from yer lands?"

Her heart pounded against her breast, for she knew where he was leading with his questions. "At least a three week ride north of me lands."

"To the north, ye say?" Almer asked, the corner of his mouth lifting ever so slightly.

"Aye," she whispered, willing her stomach to settle.

Almer gave a slow nod as he began pacing in front of her with his hands clasped behind his back. He might *pretend* he was an all important man with a brilliant mind for deduction, but Moirra knew the truth. He was an arrogant fool.

"Pray tell me then, why we found Delmar Wilgart's body some ten miles *south* of yer lands?"

Because that is where we took his pathetic dead body, ye fool! But she couldn't very well tell him the truth. "I do no' ken." She hadn't thought much about it at the time, reasoning that no one would miss Delmar. It had been a terrifying night to begin with and she hadn't been thinking clearly.

"Why would a man goin' north, to Inverness, first head *south?*" Almer asked, as if he truly cared to know the answer.

"I do no' ken," she whispered.

Almer spun and glared at Moirra. "Ye do no' ken?" he ground out. "Ye do no' ken? What *do* ye ken, Moirra Wilgart?"

The name *Wilgart* felt like an insult, a slap in the face. Moirra lifted her head and found her voice just long enough to correct him. "Me name is Moirra *McCullum,*" she said, drawing on what little energy she had left.

Almer came to stand but inches from her and leaned in. "I do no' care what ye say yer name be, ye killed me brother and for that I shall see ye hang."

He was so close that she could smell his breath. It stunk of ale and ham. The nausea roiled as bile climbed up her throat. Swallowing hard, fighting to remain calm, she looked him in the eye. "I did no' kill yer brother."

"Then who did?" he asked, his voice harsh, his words clipped.

"I do no' ken," she whispered before the world began to spin out of control.

"Ye lie!"

Almer's voice screaming at her was the last thing she remembered before the world turned black and she collapsed on the floor.

Gasps of surprise filled the room as Alysander leapt over the table where William was sitting to reach his wife. He and Deirdre arrived almost simultaneously.

He lifted her head into his lap and took her hand in his. Her skin was cold and clammy, which stood in stark contrast to the boiling anger that grew deep in his belly. "Moirra," he whispered her name repeatedly.

Deirdre took Moirra's other hand and felt for a pulse as she touched her forehead. Deirdre began searching the room with her eyes. When they locked on Almer Wilgart, she seethed. "Ye bloody fool!"

"I did no' touch her!" Almer said defensively. He stood a few steps away.

"Moirra," Alysander whispered. "Moirra, please, lass, wake up."

Soon the trio was surrounded by Moirra's daughters. "Mum!" Mariote cried out as she knelt on the floor. Esa and Muriale were in tears, hovering behind Mariote.

Alysander was not paying any attention to the back and forth taking place between Deirdre and Almer. His only concern was Moirra. He continued to plead with her to open her eyes, to not die. She lay so cold and still in his arms that his anger was suddenly replaced with fear. *What will I do without ye?*

"Deirdre," he asked, looking to her for help.

Deirdre sighed heavily before shouting for someone to bring her water and a cloth. "She made me swear no' to tell ye, Alysander."

"Tell me what?" he asked, confusion and worry etched in his face.

"She carries yer child," Deirdre explained. "She be close to three months along now."

The words hit Alysander like a blow to the chest. Pride, worry, fear, dread, and anger, all blended together in the pit of his stomach. *She carries my babe?*

He looked down at his pale, gaunt wife. Why did she want the news kept from him? The answer was simple and it shattered his heart. If she were to die, she did not want him to know she took their child with her. She was sacrificing herself and their babe to save her four daughters. Moirra knew that not much could be done to save herself without giving up Muriale, an innocent twelve-year-old girl, her own flesh and blood. His anger and grief intensified.

When Deirdre next spoke, her voice bordered on murderous. "Almer Wilgart, if this woman dies, her death will be on yer head. Ye ken she didna kill Delmar!"

"I ken no such thing, woman!" Almer shouted over the din of excitement that was building in the room. "I do no' ken why and I do no' rightly care, but she killed him as sure as I be standin' here!"

Finnis had left his seat and was now crouched down to gain a better look at Moirra. Having enough of the arguing between Almer and Deirdre, he shouted, "Enough! Enough, I say!"

All eyes turned to Finnis, whose face had turned a dark shade of red. His anger was unmistakeable. "Take her back to her cell," he told Deirdre.

"Nay!" Mariote and Esa shouted in unison. "She's ill!"

"I ken she's ill," he told the two girls, the edge not quite erased from his voice. " We will take her back to her cell so the healer can tend to her better, without all these eyes upon her."

Deirdre let go of Moirra's hand and stood. "M'laird," she began calmly, "if ye send Moirra back to that filthy cell, she will surely die before dawn." She paused to let her words sink in. "They feed her nothing but bread and the occasional bit of cheese. The cell is cold and wet. Moirra is with child and she will certainly die if Almer continues to treat her so poorly."

Almer stepped forward, his anger barely under control. "I treat her no differently than any other murderer!"

Deirdre spun to face him. "Moirra would no' kill anyone and ye well know it!"

"My brother did no' kill himself, ye bloody fool!" Almer shouted back. Spittle formed in the corner of his mouth. "I warned him she'd be the death of him, but he would no' listen! She killed him! I ken she killed him!"

While Deirdre and Almer argued, Alysander had remained on the floor, cradling his wife in his lap. She carried *his* babe. Nay, *their* babe. If he didn't do *something* and do it quickly, Moirra would die. Either by hanging or from the ill treatment she had received these past weeks. Either way, she would be dead in a matter of hours.

Tears welled in his eyes as his heart continued to splinter inside his chest. Moirra and her daughters had given him the most precious gift any man could ever ask for. They had given him a *home*. The one thing he had longed for since he was a boy and his mother died. These women had filled the dark emptiness that had at one time consumed him. Love, hope, and a real family, a family who cared so deeply for one another that they were willing to either kill or die in order to protect one another.

Alysander had not received that same kind of devotion from his own blood kin, at least not since his mother's death. If Moirra died, he knew nothing in his life would ever be the same. Her death would destroy her four daughters. It would destroy him.

Without Moirra, his life was not worth living.

He looked up at the three oldest daughters of Moirra Dundotter McCullum. Tear streaked faces and eyes filled with worry and pain stared back at him. Muriale swallowed hard, swiped away a tear, and turned away. She was walking toward the dais. Alysander knew then what her intent was and it shook him to his very soul.

In that infinitesimal moment between one heartbeat and the next, he knew what he must do.

Tenderly, he kissed Moirra's cheek, wiped a tear from his own, and stood to his full height. Looking to Finnis, he said, "Moirra did no' kill Delmar Wilgart."

His voice had been low, yet firm, and drew everyone's attention away from Deirdre and Almer. Finnis stood to face his friend. He had the sneaking suspicion that his friend was about to do something quite foolish.

"Moirra did no' kill Delmar," he said again, his voice growing in volume and strength. "I did."

ELEVEN

Astonished gasps broke out in waves across the room. Almer was frozen in place, his face a blend of incredulity and fury. "Ye lie," he ground out as he went to stand before Alysander. "Ye lie!"

Mariote, Esa and Muriale all rushed forward to plead with Alysander. "Please, ye canna do this!"

Alysander turned away from the dais and drew the girls in to his chest. He hugged them tightly for a long moment, all the while Almer pleaded with Finnis to put an end to what he referred to as a travesty of justice.

"Mariote," Alysander whispered, "please, take care of yer mum. Ye ken why I do this, lass. I can no' let yer mum sacrifice herself and our babe fer somethin' she didna do."

Mariote choked on a sob. "But ye didna do it either!" she pleaded.

He hugged her again. "Please, Mariote, take yer sisters from here. Wait outside for Deirdre, please."

"Nay, Alysander!"

He smiled, kissed the top of each of their heads and smiled. "Please, do no' argue. Yer mum needs ye more than me." He hugged them once again before turning back to face Finnis.

"Alysander," Finnis said as he did his best to hide his true feelings. "Are ye sayin' *ye* killed Delmar Wilgart?"

Alysander lifted his head and stood tall and proud. "Aye, I am."

"Ye lie!" Almer shouted angrily. "Yer only sayin' this to save yer worthless wife!"

The ends of his patience had been reached. Blinded with fury, Alysander drew back his fist and hit Almer Wilgart in his arrogant face. Blood spurted from the man's nose as he fell backward and onto the floor. Before Alysander could hit him again, four men were wrestling him to the floor.

While the sheriff's men were getting Alysander under control, William, who had yet to say a word, scooped Moirra into his arms and removed her from the room. Deirdre, and Moirra's daughters were right behind him.

Having heard no protests or calls to halt, William left the building and headed for the public stables. Once there, he propped Moirra up between Deirdre and Mariote long enough to mount his horse. "We'll take her to our cottage," he said as he lifted Moirra up and sat her on his lap.

"But they've no' set her free yet," Mariote reminded him.

William smiled down at her. "I do no' truly care," he said. "I made a promise to Alysander and I intend to keep it." Shivering and mumbling incoherently, he pressed Moirra's head against his chest. "For the love of Christ, get her daughters out of here at once," he told Deirdre.

Without uttering another word, William tapped the flanks of his horse and headed out of the village.

Once some semblance of control was regained, Finnis returned to the dais and banged the block of wood against the table. Almer's nose had finally stopped bleeding and Finnis thought he looked like a man bordering that fine line between sanity and madness.

Alysander stood with his hands bound behind his back, looking quite determined to either proceed with his earlier proclamation of guilt or to kill Almer should he say another disparaging word against his wife. Finnis gave an inward shake of his head. He was quite certain his friend had lost his mind, for he could not come up with another reason for his behavior.

"Alysander," Finnis said, his voice breaking through the silence that had filled the room. "Why do ye confess to this crime?"

Alysander pulled his shoulders back and looked Finnis directly in the eyes. "I canna let me wife hang fer a crime she did no' commit."

Before Finnis could comment or ask another question, Almer was in a rage again. "He lies! He was nowhere near Glenkirby when me brother went missin'!"

Alysander ignored his statement. "I fell in love with Moirra and wanted her for meself. She did no' ken I felt that way about her, but I knew she'd no' break her promise to Delmar. So I killed him so I could have her."

"Bah!" Almer said with a shake of his head. "How did ye kill him?"

"I shoved a dirk in his back," Alysander answered without looking at him. "Then I took him some ten miles or so south of Moirra's home and buried him in a shallow grave."

"Ye only ken that because ye learned it this day," Almer growled, his face turning purple with anger.

"Nay," Alysander said calmly. "Ye only told us *where* the body was found, not how 'twas buried." He had basically recounted the story Mariote and Muriale and told him weeks ago, after Moirra had been arrested. Alysander had information that Almer didn't and that gave him a distinct advantage. Or, at least, he hoped it did. The rest of what he knew he kept to himself. If he divulged too much, he worried it could be used against Moirra at some future time.

"So ye killed Delmar so ye could have Moirra to yerself?" Finnis asked.

"Aye."

"And Moirra had no knowledge beforehand, of what ye felt or what ye planned?"

"Moirra did no' ken anythin' beforehand." That much was true. Moirra hadn't an inkling that Delmar Wilgart was a coward who preyed on innocent young lasses.

Finnis let out a long, frustrated sigh. He knew he was being lied to. There was no doubt in his mind that there was much more to this story than he was being told. "Ye realize ye could hang fer this?"

Alysander nodded again. "Aye, I do."

If Finnis was correct in his assumption, the King's cousin was a fool who was completely willing to die to save his wife. Finnis did not believe there was a woman on this earth worth dying for.

"Alysander McCullum," he said as he sat forward in his chair. "Ye shall be held here in Glenkirby—"

Almer stepped forward, appalled and angry. "Ye canna mean to accept this man's word!"

Finnis shot to his feet and leaned over the table. "Almer Wilgart, if I hear one more word out of yer mouth this day, I swear I'll have ye bound, gagged, and thrown into the cell next to Alysander!"

Almer was not a complete fool. He clamped his mouth shut and stepped away from the dais.

"Alysander, ye shall be held here indefinitely, until we are able to sort this all out."

Almer started to speak, thought better of it and took yet another step back.

Finnis looked directly at Almer when next he spoke. "If anything happens to Alysander, I will hold ye personally responsible. He may well have admitted guilt in the murder of yer brother, but remember, he is *still* the King's cousin. Do no' forget that."

Finnis did not wait for any response from anyone else as he left the dais. He stopped halfway down the steps to give one final order. "I hereby release Moirra McCullum as well. She shall remain free until my return."

TWELVE

At first, Moirra had no idea where she was or how she came to be there. However, she did remember most of the events of the morning. She could remember her daughters' dejected faces when they'd seen her for the first time in weeks. She could also remember Alysander, looking just as dejected, just as despondent, even though he tried to paint a smile for her. What happened after that was a nonsensical blur.

When she opened her eyes, she saw Deirdre sitting on a little stool next to the small bed. When she tried to sit up, Deirdre gently pushed her back. "Wheesht, Moirra," Deirdre whispered. "Ye need to rest."

"I need a bath," Moirra argued. "And I need to get to me daughters."

"I ken ye need a bath. William and Phillip are fillin' the tub below stairs. I only ask that ye rest until it be ready."

Too tired and cold to argue, she let her head fall against the pillow. "I fear ye'll need to burn these bed coverin's, fer God only kens what be crawlin' on me clothes or in me hair."

Deirdre giggled slightly and smiled. "That be why I put ye in Thomas' bed."

Moirra closed her eyes as she felt a wave of nausea roll over her. "I was never this sick with me girls," she whispered.

"Then it must be a boy ye carry," Deirdre said softly as she dipped a clean cloth in the basin. "Or mayhap it be just because ye carry Alysander McCullum's child."

Moirra was too tired to comment, but had to agree that either one or both were strong possibilities. Deirdre wrung out the cloth and began to wipe Moirra's face and neck.

"Deirdre, where be me daughters and Alysander?" Moirra asked, her voice growing softer, weaker.

"Do no' worry over them now, Moirra. Ye've a fever and ye need to rest. They be well and ye'll see them soon. Fer now, we must concentrate on gettin' ye better."

"And clean," Moirra mumbled before drifting off to sleep again.

When she finally woke some few hours later, she was surprised to find that she had not only been bathed, but was now snuggled deep into a warm bed. Deirdre sat beside her, holding her hand. Moirra tried to sit up, but the action made her head spin. "What happened?" she asked, her throat and mouth feeling quite dry.

A relieved smile formed on Deirdre's face. "Och, lass! Ye gave us quite a scare."

"How did I get here?"

Deirdre's smile waned ever so slightly. "Finnis set ye free."

Moirra tried to shake the cobwebs from her mind. "Free?" she asked. "Why? How?"

"Wheest," Deirdre whispered. "Do no' fash yerself over it now. Ye need to rest and regain yer strength."

Moirra's stomach began to feel queasy again. She rested a hand there, fear tightening deep in her chest.

"Yer babe be fine," Deirdre reassured her. "As long as ye stay abed and try to eat, ye shall be having that babe come spring."

Moirra let out a relieved sigh. "Where is Alysander?" she asked.

The bath was meant to help break the fever as well as wash the weeks worth of gaol filth away. Though Deirdre had sworn to her that the water was as hot as Hades, Moirra thought it felt as cold as ice against her skin. Or was that the second bath? The fever was muddling her thoughts, her memories, and it made her feel angry and frustrated.

How many hours had passed since leaving the gaol, she did not know. All she knew was that her daughters and Deirdre were hovering over her like mother hens above their chicks. Where was Alysander? Why did she feel so cold? The world around her was a blurry mess. Her head pounded, her eyes throbbed, and every muscle and bone ached with an intensity she could not remember experiencing before.

"Where be Alysander?" she asked. "Me girls? Where be me girls?"

"Wheest, Moirra," Deirdre said, urging her to not worry and to try to rest.

"But I need them. I need Alysander," she insisted, with as much strength as she could muster.

In and out of awareness, hours seemed like moments, or were they days? Moirra lost all sense of time. The only thing she was certain of was that she felt quite ill and cold and extremely tired. She also desperately wanted to go home, to be wrapped up in Alysander's arms, to hear the soft sound of his breathing, to feel his heart beating against her own.

Home.

She hadn't truly felt at home or at peace since her parents' deaths. But with Alysander, she began to get a taste of it again and desperately wanted to hold onto it all the rest of her days. But where was he? Why wasn't he here to hold her, to take away the bone-deep cold that enveloped her? Mayhap he was busy rebuilding their cottage so that they could all go back there soon and live together again. That thought was the only one that brought her any comfort.

THIRTEEN

The fevers raged for days. So much so that the healer worried Moirra would not survive from one hour to the next. Toward the end, Deirdre did more praying than healing, for there really was nothing else she could do. She had tried cool baths, every herb known to break a fever and a few that were questionable. Nothing worked. In the end, 'twas all in God's hands and Moirra's determination to stay alive.

On the afternoon of the sixth day, Moirra started bleeding. 'Twas light at first, nothing that meant she was losing her babe. But the following day, the bleeding increased and there was nothing Deirdre could do to stop it.

"Alysander?" Moirra called out his name as well as her daughters' over and over again. The fever was relentless, unyielding.

As Deirdre applied cold clothes to Moirra's forehead and neck, she whispered words of encouragement and comfort. "Ye'll be well soon enough, Moirra. Ye'll see. Yer too stubborn to die just yet."

"Deirdre?" 'Twas Orabilis who spoke, standing in the doorway. "Will me mum die?"

Deirdre offered her a warm smile. "No' if I have anythin' to say about it. Do no' worry, child. Yer mum be a strong woman. 'Twill take more than the ague to take her from ye."

Orabilis did not look completely convinced. "It took her first husband."

Deirdre let loose a heavy breath. "Come here, Orabilis," she said as she held out one hand.

Hesitantly, the girl came to stand beside her. Deirdre wrapped her arms around her, drawing her in. "I do no' want ye to worry, Orabilis. We will get yer mum through this."

When the child withdrew, her eyes were damp. "I do no' have anyone else."

"Och! Orabilis that be no' true. Ye have yer sisters, ye have me. We will always be there fer ye, as will yer mum."

Moirra's eyes fluttered open. They were glassy from the fever. "I be no' goin' anywhere," she mumbled before closing her eyes again.

Orabilis smiled, though still wary.

"Ye see, lass?" Deirdre asked. "Ye heard it right from yer mum's own lips." She hoped her smile would offer some kind of encouragement.

"Aye," Orabilis said as she climbed onto Deirdre's lap. "But if she does no' make it, I swear to ye now that when I grow up, I will kill Almer Wilgart."

If such a declaration had been made by any other six-year-old child, Deirdre would have scoffed with disbelief. However, Orabilis Dundotter was not a typical six-year-old child. *I pray now fer any man brave enough to marry ye when yer aulder, child.*

FOURTEEN

The more Alysander paced the small confines of the gaol, the angrier he became, mostly with himself. Not for having confessed to the murder of Delmar Wilgart, but for not having done it sooner. If he had, his beautiful wife would not have had to suffer the filth and indignity of this god-forsaken place.

Moirra carries my child.

What would become of them, of their child? Alysander was doubtful that Moirra or their children would ever be able to get over the stigma of having been accused of murder. What hope did they have of living a normal existence?

It had been three days since his confession. Repeatedly, he had asked for quill and parchment so he could write to Moirra, explaining to her why he had done this. His request had been denied each time.

God's teeth how he missed her! He wondered if she had come to see him yet? Was she even well enough to do so? His experience taught him that if she had, she would have been turned away, just as he had been when their positions were reversed.

And the girls? He worried over them. Were they all now conspiring to plan his escape, or, worse yet, preparing to go to Almer and confess? He prayed that Moirra would be able to stop them from doing either.

And what of William McGregor? Alysander had hired him to act as counsel for Moirra. Had he washed his hands of the entire debacle? Alysander could think of no other reason why William had not come to speak with him yet. In truth, Alysander would not blame him if he had.

And Finnis. His one and only true friend had not come to see him, but how could he? With George and Harry watching over Alysander's every move, there was a good chance that Finnis could not risk visiting. If word spread of such a visit, the tongue-wagging would never cease. If anyone learned of their friendship, Finnis might very well end up being in danger of being hung right next to Alysander. If the townspeople grew angry enough, or were worked into a frenzied state of hatred, who knew what they might do. He could well imagine Almer Wilgart working the crowd into a state of frenzy and hysteria.

Nay, for now, it remained safest for Finnis to stay away, for everyone he loved to stay away.

The not knowing what was happening outside the walls of the gaol was the worst part of his incarceration. Being secluded, kept away, left his mind to wonder hither and yon for hours a day. Fretting and worrying over his wife and their babe and his stepdaughters, uncertain what would become of any of them, and knowing he could most likely hang at any moment, ate away at his confidence and hope.

How could he help his family from inside the gaol? How could he ensure they had a future without him? A future where Moirra would not have to be forced to handfast or marry yet another man? 'Twas doubtful any man would ever be inclined to marry her. Guilt tightened around his heart for finding comfort in knowing she'd never marry again. The thought of her in the arms of another man was enough to send him into a fit of rage.

Raking his hands through his hair in frustration, he went to stand under the small window. The rain had let up a few hours ago and now the sun shone brilliantly, or what he could see of it. How many more sunrises would he watch before they hung him? How many sunsets? Would he ever see Moirra again?

Nay, he didn't want her to be there when they hanged him. He would beg again for parchment and quill or for William to come to the gaol so he might make his last wishes known.

Moirra.

She had been the single best thing that had ever happened to him. Moirra and her daughters had shown him what a real and honest family was—so completely opposite his upbringing, especially after his mother passed away. He was thankful, wholly thankful for the little time he had been given with Moirra and her daughters. That was the one thing he would take with him to the gallows: the sweet, blissful memories of his time with them.

He could go in peace knowing he had experienced the love of his wife, the love of daughters he now considered his own.

William McGregor was not an uneducated or foolish man. He wished he could say the same for Alysander McCullum. While Alysander might be educated, he was as big a fool as any William had ever known. Still, he considered him a friend of sorts. And when he saw how happy Alysander made Moirra? Well, that was enough to raise his opinion of the man.

But when Alysander confessed to murdering Delmar Wilgart, William knew, beyond a shadow of a doubt, that the man was both insane and in love. A deadly combination as ever there was.

So when Finnis enlisted his aid in helping to ensure Alysander was released, William was eager to help. He would do almost anything to make certain Moirra was happy. If her husband were hanged? There would be no getting over that loss.

William had loved Moirra Dundotter ever since he was a lad of five. She had been such a kind, sweet little girl who had grown into a fine woman. There had been a time when he would have married her if he possessed the courage to ask.

But time changes people, and for that, he was thankful. He'd been happily married now for three years, the father of one bright, beautiful son with another child on the way. He adored his wife, Joanna, and the little family they'd begun. Though he still held a special, secret place in his heart for Moirra, he now looked upon her as a second sister. He adored her just as much as he adored and cherished his sister Deirdre and would do anything he could to protect either one of them.

Joanna knew that at one time William had more than just a friendly, brotherly liking for Moirra, but she also knew she had been the woman to win his heart. One of the things Joanna said she loved most about him was his strong sense of duty and family. Therefore, when he went to her three days past to let her know he would be gone for a few weeks, she did not argue. Instead, she helped him pack, making certain he had clean clothes and enough food to feed an army. But she made him promise he'd be back before she gave birth to their next child. He had four weeks. 'Twas enough to make a man go mad, being away from his wife and family and having the fate of another man's life resting on his shoulders.

Now, he was on his way to Stirling with a letter from Finnis Malcolm that he was to personally hand-deliver to Robert II. If meeting with the Guardian of Scotland wasn't enough to make a man shite his pants, then nothing would.

Riding with him were two of Finnis's men, Bruce and Alec. While they had much experience in all this riding back and forth, the politics of being in the King's court and the like, William did not. Until the past few weeks, he had been a simple man, a crofter, leading a simple life. Now, he was thrust into the center of what could only be described as insanity.

Bruce and Alec, men of dark hair and quiet demeanor, said very little as they rode like demons across the countryside. William supposed that was best, for what would they have to talk about? They came from such different backgrounds.

Once this was all over, he swore he would never allow himself to be embroiled in someone else's battle. Unless of course it was someone in his immediate family; then there would be no hope for him.

The only exception would be if it were his eldest brother Thomas. Nay, if Thomas got himself into trouble, there was a strong possibility William would allow him to hang. He reckoned most of the Moirra and Alysander's problems at the moment had come from Thomas and his dark soul. 'Twas a sorry thing a man had to say about his own brother, but 'twas true just the same. Thomas McGregor was a cruel bastard.

He hadn't always been that way. Nay, there had been a time when Thomas was a good, decent man. But their father had literally beat all the goodness out of him. For that, William was truly sorry. They had all been the recipient of Phillip McGregor's heavy hand and dark heart, but Thomas had suffered the worst, even as he grew into a young man. Phillip the senior, for whom Phillip the younger had been named, was as bitter and angry a man as William had ever seen. It wasn't discipline he meted out, but cruel, harsh punishment.

How they'd all survived was anyone's guess. Divine intervention, William supposed.

FIFTEEN

"Thank God," Deirdre whispered when she saw Moirra soaked with sweat. "The fever breaks."

Thomas was standing in the doorway to his chamber and, as always, his face bore his all-too-familiar scowl. "Good," he said. "Put her in the barn so I can have me bloody bed back."

If he wasn't Deirdre's brother she might hate him more than she did. As she dipped a cloth into the basin, she glanced up. "I'd ask if ye have a heart but I already ken the answer."

Thomas was not fazed in the least by her insult. "I want me bed back."

"Ye'll get it back when Moirra is better," she told him as she wiped Moirra's brow.

"And when will that be?"

Deirdre hadn't slept for more than a few hours at a time in days, had rarely left Moirra's side; therefore, her patience was as thin as a spider web. "Me thinks ye need to visit the brothel in Glenkirby, fer yer behavin' like a bastard right now." If anyone on God's earth needed a woman, 'twas Thomas. However, Deirdre couldn't think of anyone strong enough to put up with him, kind enough to bring back the sweet boy he had once been, and no one she disliked enough to put the task to. 'Twas a conundrum.

"I want me bed back," he repeated, a little harsher than before.

Deirdre was glad Moirra was sleeping so she wouldn't be subjected to Thomas' cold heart. She continued to wash Moirra's face and hands, pretending she hadn't heard her brother.

"Take her back to her own home," he said.

Deirdre rolled her eyes and shook her head in disgust. "What home would that be? The one that was practically destroyed by fire?"

He shrugged his shoulders. "I didna start the fire," he said. "And she be no' my responsibility, remember?"

Exasperated, Deirdre glared at him. "'Tis a good thing our mum did no' live to know the man ye've become. 'Twould have broken her heart to see ye so cold and heartless."

"Ye can thank Moirra Dundotter fer that," Thomas spat out. "She destroyed me when she refused to marry me."

Deirdre had reached the ends of her patience. Shooting to her feet, she tossed the cloth into the basin and stomped toward him. "Moirra did no' do that to ye, our father did! Now get out of here before I take a *sgian dubh* to ye!" With that, she pushed him out of the room, slammed the door shut and barred it.

"There be some comfort in knowin' he has no' changed whilst I was ill," Moirra whispered in a scratchy voice.

Deirdre felt her face grow hot with embarrassment. Quickly, she went to sit beside Moirra and placed the back of her hand on her forehead. "I think yer fever has finally broken," she said, hoping to avoid the topic of Thomas altogether.

Moirra closed her eyes and nodded slightly. "I never meant to hurt Thomas."

Deirdre's heart tightened in her chest. "Moirra, ye need no' worry about it. 'Twasn't ye who turned Thomas into the angry wretch he has become. He did that all by himself." She picked up the wet cloth, wrung it out, and went back to cleaning Moirra's face and hands. "We'll no' speak of it again. I need ye to rest now."

Moirra nodded as she took in a deep steadying breath. "I do feel verra tired, Deirdre."

"Ye've been through much these past days," she said as she patted her friend's hand.

Moirra took another steadying breath. "I lost me babe."

When she woke, Moirra realized almost immediately that something terrible had happened. Her belly felt quite empty and cold. 'Twas eerily similar to how her stomach felt after giving birth to each of her daughters, but this time, there was no joy to be found, no babe to love. Deirdre's silence was answer enough.

A tremendous ache wrapped around her heart. Any attempt to stop the tears was pointless. They streamed down her cheeks without restraint. An overwhelming sense of guilt blended with the heartache and turned her silent tears into sobs. "'Tis all me fault," she choked out.

Deirdre wrapped her hands around Moirra's. "Nay! Do no' be thinkin' that. The fault lies with Almer Wilgart and no one else."

Moirra disagreed but was too overwrought to express herself. Had she never agreed to handfast with Delmar Wilgart, none of this would be happening. She was the one who brought the man into her life and the lives of her daughters. She was the one who was so stubborn and determined to keep her farm that she could not see beyond that one singular goal. Nay, the fault lay at her feet and hers alone.

Deirdre did her best to make Moirra see the truth of the matter. "Had Almer no' been so filled with hatred toward ye, then ye'd never have been accused of killin' Delmar and ye'd never have been locked in gaol. Please, do no' blame yerself fer this."

Aye, if, if, if ... Moirra wondered silently how differently her life would be now had she never lost her first husband to begin with. But then she might not have Orabilis. And she would never have met Alysander.

Alysander.

Where was he? Mayhap he had already learned of her failure and could not bear to be near. Mayhap he was too disappointed in her.

"Where be Alysander?" she finally managed to ask.

An odd expression passed over Deirdre's face, one that added to Moirra's worry. "Somethin' has happened to him," she said as she fought to sit up.

"Alysander be well," Deirdre said as she tried to gently coax Moirra to rest. "Do no' worry over it."

Do no' worry over it? Moirra's heart sank to her belly. Instinct told her that something was wrong, very wrong.

"Where is he?"

Deirdre took a deep breath before answering. "Before I tell ye, I need yer promise no' to get upset."

That wasn't very likely.

"He confessed to killin' Delmar and now he be in gaol." Deirdre spoke so rapidly that Moirra had to ask her to repeat herself.

"Nay!" Moirra exclaimed. "Why? I do no' understand."

"Wheesht, now, Moirra," Deirdre told her. "He will be well. William has gone to Stirling with Finnis Malcolm's men to speak with Robert II. I do no' ken any more than that. William should be back within a week. We believe because Alysander is cousin to King David that he will be set free."

Of all the idiotic things Alysander could have done ...

"Why would he confess? He was no' even here when Delmar was killed," she said, sounding much confused.

A warm smile spread across Deirdre's face. "Because he loves ye, ye silly woman! He could no' stand the thought of ye bein' in that gaol one moment longer."

Alysander loved her enough that he was willing to hang for something he did not do. He loved her enough to take her place in gaol. Just because he was cousin to King David did not mean a thing at the moment. David was being held prisoner by the English. How could he possibly help from his current position?

The tears returned in full force. Not only had she lost their babe, she now might lose the only man she had ever truly loved.

SIXTEEN

It took William, Bruce and Alec six days to reach Stirling. They arrived after dawn, travel worn, covered from head to toe in mud, muck and road grime. William fully expected them to be mistaken for miscreants and turned away the moment they arrived at the gates of Stirling Castle Hence his complete surprise when they were quickly waved inside.

Young men came to retrieve their horses. Up the large stone steps and inside the castle, Bruce led them to a room where they were able to wash most of the road grime away and dust off their clothes and boots. They didn't dally, neither did they waste time in frivolous conversation, mostly because William was so terrified, he was mute. Never in his life did he ever think he would be on such an important mission, let alone seeking an audience with the Guardian of Scotland. He nearly shook with a blend of nervous anticipation and fear.

Apparently neither Bruce nor Alec suffered from the same affliction. They bounded down the hallways of Stirling as if they were Robert's own sons. They passed by many men and women as they wound their way through narrow corridors into wider ones, up staircases and through doorways. By the time they reached their destination—the only way William knew they had arrived was their sudden appearance just inside a large, well appointed room—he was out of breath and completely lost. He doubted he'd ever be able to find his way out again without a guide.

"Give me Finnis's message," Bruce said, hand held out.

Reluctantly, William removed the scroll from inside his tunic and placed it in the man's open palm.

"Stay here," Bruce said just before he and Alec left William standing in stunned and anxious silence. They disappeared behind a large carved wooden door. William was too afraid to move.

Exhausted, he could very well have fallen asleep standing upright, but his nerves would not allow for such a luxury. Time slowed to a slow crawl as he waited; he wasn't sure if it hadn't stopped altogether.

Some time passed, and William knew 'twasn't his imagination that made him think so. He had no idea what was taking place behind that door. The only sound he could make out was the pounding of his own heart beating uneasily against his chest. With no fire in the hearth, the room was cold and seemed to grow colder with each passing moment. He imagined he could very well turn into a human icicle before anyone remembered he was here.

Just when he was convinced he had in fact been forgotten, the door opened and Alec stepped through. "Come with me," he said, holding the door open.

William swallowed hard and willed his feet to move. Moments later, he was standing just inside the grandest room he had ever seen.

Heavy, meticulously crafted rugs lined the floor, tapestries hung on the walls. Tall, wide windows lined one side; in front of that was an enormous, intricately carved wooden table and behind it, an even more intricately carved chair. Ornate sconces with candles were mounted on either side of the large hearth that took up another wall. Padded chairs and tables of varying sizes were placed about the room.

The room was fit for a king though at the moment it was reigned over by Robert II, Guardian of Scotland. He was standing in front of the tall bank of windows, looking out at the yard below.

Robert II was nothing at all as William had imagined. Though he was an imposing figure, William supposed it had to do more with *who* the man was rather than his build.

Slender, with a hawkish nose and brown hair, what struck William most was how the man carried himself, standing tall and regal. One wouldn't know he had the fate of Scotland resting on his shoulders, let alone the lives of countless men, women, and children.

William stepped forward but kept what he believed was a safe and appropriate distance. He gave Robert a bow, righted himself and waited.

"How fares Finnis Malcolm?" Robert asked after giving William a quick glance up and down.

His voice was deep and not at all what William expected. "He fares well, me laird," William answered, hoping no one noticed the slight crack in his voice.

"And how fares David's cousin, Alysander McCullum? Is he well?"

William couldn't hide his surprise. Until this very moment, he had thought Alysander's claim of being related to the king was at best, an exaggeration. "Not well, me laird," William said after regaining his senses.

"Explain," Robert said, clasping his hands behind his back.

William thought it an odd question considering why they were here. "He be in gaol, in Glenkirby, me laird," William replied with the belief that no further explanation was needed. He was quite wrong.

"I ken verra well that he is in gaol. I want to ken how he fares."

William cleared his throat before going into what he hoped was enough detail to make Robert's scowl disappear. "Well, he misses his wife somethin' fierce, ye ken—"

"So 'tis true then. He has married?"

"Aye, me laird, he has. A fine woman she be. I've known her me whole life and ne'er a finer woman ye'll find, save fer me own wife, ye ken."

Robert's scowl was replaced with a warm smile, but he remained quiet and listened intently to William's description. "Moirra Dundotter she be," he said as he offered up his own smile. "She be a good woman, me laird, and I ken without a doubt that she did no' kill Delmar Wilgart."

Robert quirked a curious brow and asked, "How can ye be so certain?"

William was firm in his answer. "Ye'd have to ken Moirra Dundotter."

Robert cast a furtive glance at Bruce before speaking again. "I be told the sheriff believes she killed this Delmar Wilgart person for his bag of coin."

William scoffed at that notion. "Moirra has more wealth than Delmar Wilgart ever thought to possess. She did no' need his money. What she needed was his strong back in helping her with her farm."

Robert gave that idea a measure of thought. "So ye say she would no' have killed him fer his coin?"

William let out a frustrated breath. "I be sayin' she'd no' kill a man fer *any* reason, me laird."

"No' even to protect herself from harm?"

"Would no' yer own wife or daughters?" He hadn't meant for his answer to sound insolent or disrespectful and hoped Robert did not take it that way.

"I be also told that there be a good deal of corruption amongst the sheriff and his men. Be this true?" Robert asked, ignoring William's question.

"Aye, there be much corruption," William answered. "Almer Wilgart and his men make the merchants pay fer their protection against thieves and the like, but a lot of good it does them. The merchants pay fer protection but Almer pays thieves to steal from them. He keeps what he wants, then sends his men off to Edinburgh or Aberdeen to sell the rest."

Robert looked to Bruce and Alec for confirmation. Alec nodded in affirmation whilst Bruce said, "I believe he speaks the truth."

Robert began to pace back and forth in front of those lavishly adorned windows. William waited as patiently as he could whilst Robert was lost in thought. After some time, Robert turned his attention back to William.

"Why did Alysander confess to killin' this Delmar Wilgart?" he asked.

William let out a long, heavy breath before answering. "Do I have permission to speak candidly, me laird?"

"Aye, ye do."

William cleared his throat and chose his words as carefully as he could under the circumstances. "I believe he be tetched."

A long moment passed before Robert, Bruce and Alec broke out into a fit of boisterous laughter. William felt much relieved to know he hadn't insulted anyone.

"Aye," Robert said as he struggled to regain his composure. "Alysander McCullum be tetched. Of that, there be no doubt."

It took a few moments, but the laughter finally subsided. "William, tell me yer opinion on the matter of Alysander McCullum's confession," Robert said.

In William's mind, 'twas a simple explanation. "Alysander confessed to get his wife out of gaol. She be carryin' his child, ye see—"

Robert cut him off in mid sentence. "Alysander McCullum is going to be a father?" He was clearly surprised.

"Aye," William answered. "But when I left, she was verra ill, thanks to Almer and that filthy hovel he calls his gaol. Me sister Deirdre was tendin' to Moirra when I left."

Anger flickered in Robert's eyes, albeit briefly. "I do no' ken Alysander as well as I do Finnis Malcolm." He crossed the small space and retrieved Finnis's parchment from the top of his desk. "Apparently, Finnis agrees with yer assessment of the situation." He tapped the parchment against one hand a few times before speaking again. "I will need time to think on this. Ye'll have me decision shortly."

With that, Bruce escorted William out of the room and back into the small chamber. There was nothing left for him to do at this moment other than pray.

SEVENTEEN

Thankfully, William was not forced to wait long. Within a few short hours, he had Robert's answer, as well as three rolled parchments containing the guardian's decision on the matter of Alysander and Moirra McCullum. Before the day was out, William, Bruce and Alec had fresh horses, packs full of food, and much lighter hearts as they headed out of Stirling to return to Glenkirby.

William could only pray that they reached the village before Almer's patience wore thin and he hanged Alysander and Moirra out of spite.

It took two days longer to get home than it did to get to Stirling. Torrential rains impeded any good progress they might have been able to make. The longer they were delayed the more ill-tempered William became. 'Twas beyond frustrating to know that a man's life rested in the palm of your hands, or in this case, within the writing on a parchment tucked inside his tunic, and you might be delayed in helping to save his life all because of rain.

'Twas relentless.

'Twas downright maddening.

One of the paths that ran through a glen had been washed away, forcing them to slog through mud up to the horses' knees. And the rain continued to fall, the skies remained dark and sullen. But still, they trudged on, determined to make it to Glenkirby before Almer Wilgart did something that could not be undone.

EIGHTEEN

It had been nearly a year since Connor McCullum had seen his brother, Alysander.

When he left, right after their brother Hugh died, Connor was certain he'd never see Alysander again. Hugh had been killed in drunken brawl and Alysander might as well have been declared dead as well, as far as their father was concerned. It pained Connor to think he had lost two brothers that fateful day. It pained him just as much to learn that Alysander was in gaol in Glenkirby, set to be hanged for murder.

Much had changed within the McCullum clan these many months and there was a good chance Alysander knew nothing of those changes. Knowing his brother as he did, however, he suspected those adjustments would change nothing concerning how Alysander felt about himself or his family.

Connor's love of his brother precluded him from doing nothing or remaining silent on the matter. No matter what Alysander believed, Connor and their brother, Archibald *did* love him. Neither Connor nor Archibald held any ill-will toward him. Nay, 'twas in fact quite the opposite. It had been their father who behaved so hatefully toward Alysander, not them. But he had been too overwrought with grief and guilt to see the truth.

What exactly had happened to him, how he ended up in a filthy gaol, Connor could only begin to guess. No doubt copious amounts of alcohol had been involved. His brother was no stranger to drink. Nay, 'twas more like Alysander and drink were the best of friends. The stories of Alysander's drinking were legendary and, after he left, the stories continued on for months. Eventually, however, they stopped hearing the rumors and they no longer heard about their fabled brother.

Until a week ago, Connor had begun to believe his brother had either drunk himself to death or had been killed in a drunken brawl as Hugh had been.

Then he received word from Finnis Malcolm.

The missive had been quite brief.

Alysander is being held in the gaol in Glenkirby, accused of murder. Please come at once.

Those two small sentences were enough to make Connor's blood run cold.

What had his brother gotten himself into this time? There was only one way to find out and that was to go to Glenkirby. Connor could only pray he would arrive in time to keep the hangman's noose from being placed around Alysander's neck.

NINETEEN

'Twas no secret that Thomas McGregor despised Moirra Dundotter.
'Twas also no secret that at one time, long ago, he had loved her.
But she had destroyed him with one simple word: *nay*.
Nay she did not love him, nay she wouldn't marry him and nay, she'd not sell her farm to him.
As children, they had been good friends. Up until the day she married her first husband, Kenneth McPherson. Thomas hadn't held that union against Moirra, for he knew 'twas all his fault for being too much a coward to ask for her hand.
Then Kenneth had died from an ague and his hope for finally winning her hand burned bright.
Thomas had waited a full year, giving her time to mourn Kenneth, before asking for her hand. What had she done? She smiled that sweet smile of hers and told him 'nay'. "I canna marry a man I do not love. I love ye as a friend, like a brother, Thomas, but I canna marry ye."
Her refusal, hidden behind sweet words and sweeter smiles, nearly did him in.
Then she married a second time, to some man whose only attribute was his broad shoulders. But Moirra seemed quite smitten with him. Thomas wished her all the best, hiding his heartbreak behind a facade of indifference. By that time, Thomas' father had turned harder, his hands harsher, even though Thomas was full-grown. Never a crueler man walked the earth than Phillip McGregor. It had been that way since Thomas was a boy and only grew worse as he got older.
Thomas hid his pain and embarrassment from everyone, even into adulthood. His brothers and sister knew how cruel Phillip could be, but they didn't know the half of it. Thomas learned early on how to take a

beating without crying out or begging for mercy, for neither would do him a damned bit of good. "Why ye be walkin' so oddly," one of his brothers would ask. Thomas would lie and say he tripped and twisted his ankle or fell down and landed on a rock, or some other ridiculous lie, just to hide the truth. He didn't lie to save his father's reputation. Nay, he lied to hide his humiliation.

The last time his father beat him, Thomas was just shy of two and twenty. He'd been caught off guard by a hard punch to the gut that knocked the air clean from his lungs. Thomas had tried to defend himself, but his father was bigger and angrier and that bloody strop had caught him at the back of his head, leaving him dazed. He'd only managed to get in one good punch before Phillip slammed a big fist against his jaw and sent him to the ground. When the strop tore through his tunic, then his flesh, Thomas passed out. He woke sometime later with a bloodied lip and his back torn to shreds.

The beating was punishment for not being able to get Moirra to agree to sell her land.

The old man died a month later and 'twas all Thomas could do not to dance on the man's grave.

There were many times he had been tempted to either run away or kill his father. The only reason he had done neither was because of the promise he had made to his mother on her deathbed.

The land he farmed had belonged to his mother's family—land his father had gained by marrying her. Dalina McGregor had begged Thomas never to leave, never to let it fall into anyone else's hands. At the time, she had been too ill to realize what she was asking and Thomas had been too consumed with grief at her impending death to argue. So he made the promise never to leave and never, no matter how tempted he was, to kill Phillip, even though they both knew he would probably deserve it.

Too much had happened to him over the years to start anew. Thomas' heart held too much anger, resentment and humiliation for him to change into the man he had at one time desired to be. He blamed Moirra for all of it.

Had she married him the first time he had asked, his life would be so very different. There was a chance back then for him to change, to grow. He would have worshipped the very ground she walked upon, would have treated her like a queen.

But she didn't love him.

And she wouldn't sell her farm to him, no matter how many times he asked or how great an offer he made for it.

Then she handfasted with Delmar Wilgart.

Delmar. Wilgart.

If that wasn't a slap in the face, nothing was. Delmar Wilgart was a lying cheat and quite deft at manipulating women, something those unsuspecting women didn't catch on to until it was too late. Thomas imagined it was Delmar's smile and soft-spoken voice that did the trick.

When he'd learned that Moirra was handfasting with Delmar, he got drunk and stayed that way for a week. Delmar, lying, cheating son of a whore, was a better choice than him? It made no bloody sense at all. Thomas tried to warn Moirra, but she wouldn't listen. He supposed she thought he was simply jealous and only wanted her land. But that wasn't true. He wanted *her*.

Now Delmar was dead and Moirra had been accused of killing him.

Though there was no real evidence against her, Thomas had managed to convince Almer that his brother was dead by the hands of Moirra Dundotter. It had required very little effort. Almer had a very malleable mind; it also helped that he didn't like Moirra. But then, there were few women Almer did like. Thomas supposed *that* was due to the fact that so many women disliked *him*.

Finally, Thomas was able to exact a bit of vengeance against Moirra. Being accused of murder and tossed into gaol was no less than he thought she deserved for all the heartache and suffering she had caused him. There was a very miniscule part of him, just a tiny piece of his heart that did feel some measure of sadness toward her. But he pushed those thoughts and feelings down, down deep, and smothered the life out of them with his vehemence.

Moirra Dundotter got no less than she deserved.

Just when he thought he would finally see her suffering as he believed she deserved, Alysander McCullum stepped forward to confess and take her place.

Any man who would willingly sacrifice his own life for a woman, especially the likes of Moirra, deserved to be hanged.

But when rumors spread that Alysander was cousin to the king, Thomas had serious doubts the man would actually hang.

If God wouldn't see fit to take their lives, the least Thomas could do was to make their lives as miserable as possible.

The longer he was stuck inside the cold, dank gaol, the more Alysander felt his grasp on reality and any remnants of sanity begin to slip away. Worry for Moirra and their daughters was overwhelming, wreaking havoc on his mind and heart. Finnis hadn't been to see him in more than a week and neither had anyone else. Or if they had, Almer was refusing them entry.

With no news on how his wife was doing and being locked away as he was, he was left with plenty of time to conjure up all sorts of horrific images: Moirra dying and the children left all alone with no one to care for them. Another fire breaking out and no one there to help them. Their lives after he was hanged; what would their future hold then? 'Twas enough to make his heart seize whenever he thought of all the possibilities.

'Twas late in the day when he heard the heavy wooden door that separated the gaol from the public rooms open. Assuming 'twas Almer, George or Harry coming in to taunt him, he remained prone on the cot, lying on his back with his head resting on his folded arms. The three men loved to bring in their meals of venison or ham and eat them in front of Alysander, all the while licking their lips, wiping their greasy hands on their even greasier clothing. Oftentimes, they would drop bits of food on the floor and kick them his way. Alysander spent many an hour thinking about what he'd do if he were ever out of this Godforsaken place, reckoning he'd start by slamming three greasy, tooth-missing, smug faces against the thick, heavy steel bars until they bled to death.

"McCullum!" George called out as he approached the cell. "Ye've a visitor."

Believing 'twas Finnis come finally to see him, Alysander jumped to his feet excitedly and went to the bars. His excitement was short-lived when he saw Thomas McGregor approaching. His stomach fell away at the sight of the man, for Alysander was certain he was here to deliver bad news.

"Ye look like shite, McCullum," Thomas said with a hint of smugness. "Or be it Pillory John? What be they callin' ye these days?"

Moirra had named him *Pillory John* the day they first met, for Alysander had refused to tell her his real name. That had been months ago, yet it seemed a lifetime had passed since she rescued him from the town pillory. She had paid his bail in exchange for a handfasting because she needed a strong back to work on her farm. It hadn't taken long for Alysander to fall so deeply in love with her that now, he was willing to risk his own life in order to save hers.

"No matter what they call ye, ye still look like shite," Thomas said with a smile that bordered on a sneer.

Nonplussed, for he knew Thomas spoke the truth, Alysander raised a curious brow but remained mute. *Ye try livin' in gaol fer a few days,* he thought to himself. He doubted Thomas McGregor would last more than a day or two behind bars.

"I would ask how ye ffare, but from the looks and smell of ye, 'tis no' necessary," Thomas said.

Move just a few inches closer, McGregor, Alysander thought. *Just close enough fer me to get me hands around yer throat.* "What do ye want?" Alysander asked in a cool voice.

Thomas chuckled slightly as he crossed his arms over his chest. "Even behind bars fer these weeks, ye still manage to believe yer better than the rest of us." He shook his head as if he couldn't believe it possible.

Alysander refused to allow the man to goad him into losing his temper.

"Why be ye here?" he asked again.

'Twas then that a smile, quite sinister looking, formed on Thomas McGregor's lips. "Do ye ken where yer wife be?"

Alarm kicked at Alysander's gut. That god awful smile on Thomas' face sickened him.

Thomas nodded as if Alysander's silence explained everything. "I did no' think ye did," he said. "Would ye like to ken where?"

Alysander swallowed back the bile that was beginning to rise.

"At this verra moment, yer wife be in me home. In *me* bed."

Fury erupted. Alysander lunged at the bars, slamming against them with outstretched arms, just itching to wrap his hands around Thomas' throat.

Thomas simply smiled, feeling quite safe on his side of the cell. "Did ye truly think her better than that?" he asked. "I've known Moirra me whole life, McCullum. 'Tis naught fer her to go from one man to the other when it suits her."

Alysander continued to stretch his arms out, his fingers just inches away from Thomas. Fury, rage and fear blended together, clouding his good judgment. "Stay away from me wife!" he shouted.

"Do no' worry. I've no' bedded her. Yet."

Alysander wrapped his fingers around the bars and yanked hard, wanting nothing more than to tear them down and get to Thomas. "I swear, McGregor, if ye lay a hand on yer, I'll kill ye."

Thomas cocked his head to one side. "Do ye no' see, McCullum? Ye've served yer purpose with Moirra. She does no' want ye anymore. She'll be callin' an end to yer handfastin' and I will marry her."

Bile rose along with great fury, so much that Alysander's head began to spin.

"And if ye manage to not be hanged, ye can slither off to wherever it be ye came from," Thomas said, offering Alysander a slight bow and an ugly smile before quitting the room.

Thomas had to be lying, that was all there was to it. Fear, dread and uncertainty blended with anger and guilt, assaulted Alysander's mind and heart. Moirra was better than that, better than Thomas described her. Never would she sink so low as to go to that man.

Alysander thought back to the times he and Moirra had discussed Thomas McGregor. While she admitted they had been friends as children, she had also admitted to turning down his many proposals. *"Thomas was a sweet boy but somethin' happened and he grew into a cold, hard man. Though he has proposed many a time, I was no' quite desperate enough to say 'aye' to him."*

Was she desperate enough now?

That was his deepest fear. Moirra carried his babe. He was in gaol. She had four daughters to think of.

The more he considered, the more fearful and angry he became. Doubt pummeled his heart; fear tore at his soul.

Nay! He told himself. Moirra would never do such a thing. Whether he hanged or not, she would never end up in the arms of Thomas McGregor.

Would she?

Thomas had taken great delight in tormenting Alysander and he felt no guilt over it. He had one person left to see, one life left to destroy before he felt any measure of satisfaction or relief: Moirra.

He returned to his home as quickly as he could. Home was by no means a palatial estate. Nay, 'twas a simple cottage with stone floors on the lower level. Above stairs were two small rooms, one of which belonged to Thomas. At one time it had been his parents' bedchamber; now 'twas his. The other room was where he and his three brothers had slept when they were growing up. Deirdre had a tiny spot below stairs, just off the kitchen and near the hearth. By outward appearances, it was a comfortable and cozy home. Mayhap it could have been at one time, were it not for Phillip McGregor.

Thankfully, Deirdre had left to check on William's wife, Joanna, who was due to give birth to their second child very soon. The brats Moirra called her daughters were also nowhere to be seen. A tingle of excitement rushed up and down his spine when he realized he would be allowed time alone with Moirra.

Quietly, he tapped against the door to his bedchamber before stepping inside.

Moirra was sitting in bed, her back and head propped up with pillows. Dark circles had formed under her pretty green eyes. Her blond hair—hair he used to imagine cascading around her naked body as he swived her mercilessly—was twined into one thick, long braid, that tumbled across one breast, where it disappeared under a blanket. Betwixt her fingers, which rested in her lap, was a handkerchief, no doubt to dry away her tears.

If he hadn't hated her so much at that moment, he might feel sorry for her.

When she looked up to see him standing in the doorway, her eyes flickered with surprise and leeriness. He supposed that was better than the way she typically looked at him: with indifference.

"How fare ye this day, Moirra?" he asked, feigning true concern.

Moirra shrugged her shoulders. "I have been better, Thomas."

Lying through his teeth, he said, "I be sorry fer ye. First the babe and now Alysander."

Her brow knitted in confusion. "What of Alysander?"

"Has no one told ye yet?" he asked. Her gullibility made it so easy to lead her to believe he cared for her at all.

"Told me what, Thomas?"

He could see her growing more apprehensive and fearful with each moment that passed. He sighed as if it took great discomfort to muster the courage to answer. "Alysander has learned that ye lost yer babe. He has decided to go back to his clan."

Wide-eyed, stunned and bewildered, she felt tears well in her already swollen, bloodshot eyes. "Nay," she whispered, unable to believe it. "That can no' be."

"I spoke with William just this morn." 'Twas another lie, for no one had heard from William since he'd left for Stirling. Alysander was the king's cousin and Thomas thoroughly believed he would be released just as soon as William returned. Hopefully, by that time, he would have convinced Moirra that Alysander no longer wanted her. "Robert II ordered yer husband set free. Once he learned that ye lost yer babe, he left." He let his words sink into her malleable mind before going further. "I do no' ken why, Moirra. Mayhap the loss was too much for him to bear. Mayhap he spent too much time in gaol and needs to return home fer a time. I be certain once he clears his mind he will come fer ye."

He added the last part for one reason. If he said too many negative things about Alysander, Moirra would end up not believing him. But if he made it sound as though he sincerely cared, that there was hope for her and Alysander, it added to the believability of his lie.

Tears streamed down her cheeks, her shoulders shook, her face contorted into a mask of heartache and pain. Thomas went to her then, sitting on the edge of the bed. "Wheesht, now, Moirra. Do no' give up hope yet. All will be no' lost, ye ken? Ye have yer daughters, Deirdre, and believe it or no', even me. I ken ye think me nothin' more than a greedy son of a whore, but I do care what happens to ye. I always have."

"Why would he leave me? He loves me and I him. I do no' understand, Thomas."

Another heavy sigh. "Who kens what makes any man do anythin', Moirra. Mayhap ye did no' ken him as well as ye thought ye did? But it matters no'. It be no' the end of the world. Ye still have yer daughters."

Moirra shook her head and wiped away her tears. "Aye, I have me daughters."

Thomas patted her hand as he plastered a look of tender concern on his face. "I ken it might no' be the best time to discuss this, but I want ye to ken that if anything should ever happen to ye, yer daughters always have a home here. All of ye are always welcome here."

She cast him a wary look. "Why do ye behave so kindly to me now?"

Feigning a look of contrition, he said, "When I saw how ill ye were, it scared me near to death. I soon realized that I miss the friendship we used to share. I've been a fool and I can only pray ye'll fergive me someday."

Moirra studied him closely for a long moment. Thomas did his best to look contrite and sincere.

"I do fergive ye, Thomas."

'Twas all he could do not to jump to his feet and scream '*hallelujah*!' "I thank ye kindly,. And remember, no matter what happens, ye can stay here as long as ye need or want. I ken ye can no' go to yer own home just yet, fer ye need to rest and heal yerself."

"Thank ye kindly," she said. "I think I would like to be alone now, to rest and to try to sort this all out."

He gave her hand another gentle pat before quitting the room.

Below stairs, he poured himself a cup of fine whisky to celebrate. He had planted huge seeds of doubts in the minds of two people this day. He felt quite certain that the longer Moirra stayed abed, alone with her thoughts, the more her heart would break when she realized Alysander wasn't coming for her.

Now all he had to do was to think of a way to keep Alysander away when he was released. Thomas still had no doubt that the man would be freed. 'Twas just a matter of when. Hopefully, it would be days if not weeks from now. He needed time to figure out what to do next to keep Moirra and Alysander apart. The longer the seeds of doubt lay in their hearts, the better it would be for him.

So he sat in the quite stillness of the late hour and drank and thought.

When he finished his third cup of whisky, he was no closer to a plan of keeping the lovers apart than he had been earlier.

When the solution finally presented itself, a smile exploded on his face. He lifted his fourth cup of whisky and toasted the air before him. "To murder!"

TWENTY

'Twas just before dawn when William, Bruce and Alec entered the village of Glenkirby. Straightaway they went to the inn where Finnis Malcolm was staying and thundered up the steps. William pounded his fist against the wooden door repeatedly until Finnis flung it open.

"What in the bloody hell?" he asked as he stood eyes still bleary from sleep, bare-chested, wearing trews that were untied. The fog of sleep cleared almost instantly when he saw William standing in the semi-dark corridor, with Bruce and Alec on either side of him.

"I have word from Robert II," William said as he pushed his way into the room. Bruce and Alec followed.

Finnis let out a quick breath and raked a hand through his brown hair. "It be about time."

Alysander had slept very little, his thoughts plagued with doubt and worry over what Thomas McGregor had told him the night before. *Moirra is at McGregor's home. In his bed.*

He'd been in gaol for nearly three weeks with no word from anyone. With little food and even less warmth, his nerves were gone, torn asunder. Any hope to survive this ordeal, to live the rest of his days with the woman he loved beyond measure, had quickly dwindled after McGregor's visit.

Mayhap Thomas spoke the truth. Mayhap Moirra was convinced that Alysander was going to hang. Mayhap, like him, she had lost all hope. She had four daughters to think of, as well as the child—their child—that she carried. How could he blame her for doing what she must in order to survive?

The heartache was almost too much to bear. He wasn't sure if he should feel betrayed or relieved that she had moved on with her life, even if it had been only a few weeks. But, bloody hell, could she not have waited until Almer Wilgart had tied the noose around his neck?

Back and forth he went, betwixt grief and anger as it gnawed at his gut until he felt as vulnerable and weak as a newly born lamb. By the time the sun began to rise the following morning, he had no strength left to fight the demons battling inside his mind.

As he lay in the dark morning hours, he heard the heavy wooden door push open. Was it Thomas come back to insult and taunt him? *Mayhap he be here to tell me he bedded me wife*, Alysander sulked. He closed his eyes, intent on ignoring anyone who might be coming toward his cell. *To hell with all of them.*

Footsteps fell in hurried progression across the stone floor. They were the kind of footsteps that bode a warning. But who they belonged to or why they were quickly making their way toward his cell, Alysander cared not. Though instinct told him the owner of the footsteps was on a mission of some importance and mayhap 'twould be a good idea for him to prepare himself for whatever might be heading his way, Alysander continued to ignore that inner voice. He remained where he was; lying on his back in the cot, eyes closed, feet crossed at his ankles. *They've come to hang me*, he mused. *Let them.*

He'd fallen that far.

So far into the abyss of depression that he no longer cared if he lived or died. Moirra was with Thomas McGregor.

As it had been since his mother's death, Alysander McCullum was alone once again.

He had nothing left to fight for.

Connor McCullum, chief of Clan McCullum had scared the living daylights out of George when he and his entourage of ten tall, muscular, angry looking men came barging into the public room of the gaol moments ago. They were all so blasted *large* that it amazed George they all fit inside the tiny room. Connor McCullum had to have been the most imposing man George had ever met in his life. The man was tall, a good six inches taller than George. Wide-shouldered, a massive chest and arms that looked as though they'd killed more than one man in his lifetime. He wore a dark tunic over leather trews. A plaid of brown, goldenrod and green was draped over one shoulder and around his waist. He also sported a cloak made of what George was quite certain to be the fur of a black bear. He had pulled the fur back and tucked it around the hilt of his broadsword. All in all, a most terrifying image.

"I be Connor McCullum, chief of clan McCullum. I be told yer keepin' me brother, Alysander, in yer gaol."

George barely managed a nod of affirmation before the terrifying man stepped toward him.

It only took one look to discover two things. First, there was no mistaking Connor and Alysander were brothers. Two, Connor McCullum was quite angry and quite serious about slicing George's throat with the dirk he had pressed against it.

"I have more than one hundred of me men waitin' out of doors, ye ken? I will see me brother, now, little man," Connor said. "Or ye will nae live to see the sun finish rising over the horizon."

George was not as inept or foolish as some might have been led to believe. "Aye, m'laird," he squeaked out.

Connor sheathed his weapon inside his heavy leather belt, gave a quick nod and glowered fiercely at him. "Be quick about it."

George scrambled out of his chair and headed toward the heavy wooden door. His hands shook as he fumbled with a ring of iron keys, looking for the one that would unlock the door. He was fully prepared to give them the key to Alysander McCullum's cell if they asked for it, Almer Wilgart be damned.

Grabbing a lit torch from the wall, George had led the way to Alysander's cell. With a shaky hand, he held the torch up and out so Connor McCullum could see into the dark cell.

Connor took one look at his brother and shook his head. With a heavy sigh, he said, "What have ye done this time, brother?"

For a brief moment, Alysander thought he might be dreaming. He had not thought of his brother Connor much in months. Mayhap 'twas simply his mind playing tricks, now that the end of his life was drawing near. For a long moment, he did not move. He simply waited.

"Open the bloody door," Connor growled.

Next he heard the jangling of keys as one was shoved into the heavy iron lock. Alysander swallowed hard before daring to open one eye, just to peak, just to make certain 'twasn't insanity taking hold.

The door swung open and a large figure stepped inside.

Connor.

His eldest brother, the man he both admired and envied. "Connor," Alysander said as he jumped out of bed and stood before him. "Why are ye here?" He wasn't so much excited to see his brother as he was leery. They had not parted on the best of terms last year and as far as Alysander knew, he was not necessarily one of Connor's favorite people.

Connor thought it an awfully stupid question considering the circumstances. "I get word that ye be sittin' in gaol in this godforsaken place, that ye've been accused of murder, and ye ask why I be here?" He turned to George, who was still shaking with fright and said, "He asks why I be here."

When George remained mute, Connor simply shook his head and turned his attention back to Alysander. "And to think Da always considered ye the most intelligent of all his sons."

Alysander's mouth fell open. "Ye must be drunk, fer we both ken well that our father can no' stand the sight of me, least of all would he consider me to be his smartest son."

Connor's expression changed from playful to serious rather rapidly. "Alysander, much has happened since ye left, much ye do no' ken."

Connor's sudden change in countenance, as if he bore the weight of the world on his shoulders — though broad they may be — brought an overwhelming sense of unease to the pit of Alysander's stomach. Why, after all this time, he still cared about his family and his clan, he did not quite understand. Hadn't he pushed away all those kind-hearted feelings toward his brothers long ago? Again, he had to think 'twas his current predicament that left him with that sorrowful and worried feeling.

Turning to George, Connor said, "I want me brother released, and I want him released *now*."

A most peculiar expression washed over George's face as his skin turned ashen. "I-I can no' do that, m'laird. Only the sheriff or the King's emissary can do that."

Connor stepped forward, bent low so he could look George in the eye. "Then I suggest ye find either one of them and bring them here at once. Else I'll tell those one hundred and fifty men waitin' fer us outside to tear ye limb from limb."

Alysander almost—not quite, but *almost*—felt sorry for George. The man looked as though he was ready to piss his trews. Served the fool right for having been such an arse these past weeks.

George nodded rapidly before bowing and scurrying away to do Connor's bidding. Connor and Alysander smiled as the man disappeared as if his arse was on fire.

"He left the door open," Alysander said when Connor turned to face him.

"Aye, that he did," Connor said as he raised a devilish brow. "We could leave now, me brother."

Alysander gave the idea some thought before answering. "Nay, 'twould no' look good fer the future chief of Clan McCullum to be hangin' from the gallows next to his brother."

Alysander noted once again that odd expression fall across his brother's face.

"Tell me why yer here," Connor asked in a low, concerned voice.

Alysander let loose with a long, heavy sigh as he ran a hand through his brown hair. "I fear that be a very long story, Connor."

Connor smiled rather devilishly. "I do no' think we be goin' anywhere anytime soon."

Realizing his brother was probably correct in his assessment, Alysander took in a deep breath and began to explain the events that led to his being incarcerated. "It all began many months ago when I got so bloody drunk that I could no' find me arse with both hands. I was set upon by a small band of highwaymen ..."

The more Alysander told his story of how he came to be here, the wider Connor's eyes and mouth became. A wife? Four daughters? 'Twas all completely out of character for Alysander. What surprised Connor even more was the fact that Alysander had given up drinking anything stronger than cider. "I never thought I'd live to see the day *ye* gave up drink," Connor said with more than a hint of surprise in his voice.

Alysander smiled woefully. "Mayhap, had I stayed drunk, I'd no' be here today." But then he would not have met the most beautiful, kind, wonderful woman he had ever known. Neither would he be suffering from a broken heart the likes of which he would never have believed possible. *How can a man still live when his heart has been ripped from his chest?*

Cocking his head slightly and raising a brow, Connor said, "But ye've a beautiful wife from what ye tell me, as well as four daughters. Certainly they were worth givin' up the drink?"

"Aye, she be beautiful." There was no way to deny that. She was also charming, smart, witty, giving, and perfectly capable of tearing his heart to little pieces.

"Do ye love her?" Connor asked in a low voice.

Did he love her? More than he loved the next breath he would take. More than he could fathom. The fact that she was now in Thomas McGregor's bed did nothing to change how he felt about her. They could hang him this very day and he would go through eternity loving that woman. "Aye, Connor, I fear I do."

Connor was about to ask another question when a great commotion coming from the public area broke out. Moments later, Finnis Malcolm came bursting into the gaol, along with William McGregor and a handful of other men. Bringing up the rear and practically screeching like a banshee was Almer Wilgart.

"Ye can no' do this!" Almer cried out at the men walking ahead of him. "He has confessed! We are set to hang him on the morrow!"

Hang him on the morrow? Alysander hadn't been privy to that bit of information.

"I will petition the King!" Almer continued to call out to the backs of the men. "Robert II has no right to do this!"

Finnis had apparently heard enough of Almer's complaints. He spun on his heels and thundered toward him. "Would ye like me to have ye put in chains and taken to Robert so ye might tell him yerself that ye claim he has no right to do this?"

Almer went ashen for the briefest moment, as if he were thinking on Finnis's threat. The ugly scowl Alysander had grown accustomed to seeing on the man's face returned quickly. "Verra well, ye may have Alysander McCullum, but I will leave this verra moment to go to Thomas McGregor's home and retrieve Moirra Dundotter. I ken she be the one who killed me brother, no matter what Alysander claims."

William stepped forward then, bearing the fiercest and most frightening glower he could manage. "If ye step one wee little toe on me lands, I will kill ye."

Fear flickered briefly in Almer's eyes. "It be Thomas's land, no' yers."

"It be mine as much as Thomas's and I will no' warn ye again. Moirra did no' kill yer good-fer-nothin' brother!"

"That is enough," Finnis growled. "Ye've read Robert's missive," he held the missive up in one hand as a reminder to Almer. "Ye'll no' be arrestin' Moirra or anyone else fer that matter."

To say the least, Alysander was as confused as Connor seemed to be. Together, they stepped out of the cell and toward the group of men. "Pray tell," Alysander asked. "Could one of ye explain what yer all arguin' over?"

"How did ye get out of yer cell?" Almer demanded.

"Yer man did no' lock it when he went to find ye," Connor said with a nod toward George. George, who had been standing beside Almer, went as pale as a ghost. "Ye might want to have a conversation with him about the proper way to keep yer prisoners *in* gaol."

Almer began to shout at George, who seemed to shrink with each insult and threat hurled at him.

"Enough!" Finnis shouted. His face was an odd shade of deep red, a sure sign that his patience had been tested beyond its limits. All eyes in the small area turned to look at him.

He let out an exasperated sigh as he turned to face Alysander and handed him the missive. "By order of Robert II, ye are hereby declared innocent of the charges against ye. Ye'll no' be hanged on the morrow," he said as he turned to face Almer. "Or any other day."

Almer's eyes turned to slits, his anger and fury undeniable. "And what of Moirra Dundotter? Will ye let that murderin' whore go free as well?"

Simultaneously, Alysander and William lunged at Almer and tackled him to the stone floor. Alysander got to his knees and held Almer by the scruff of his tunic. "Ye'll never say such a thing about Moirra ever again, Almer Wilgart!"

"Do no' hit him, Alysander," William warned as he too got up on his knees. "Ye've been in enough trouble these many days."

While it made every bit of sense to *not* hit Almer and end up in more trouble, the urge to ignore William's warning was almost too great. But before he could make the decision, William made it for him.

"But me?" William said as he smiled down at Almer. "I have no such troubles." And with that, he slammed his huge fist into Almer's face. The sound of Almer's nose breaking was music to Alysander's ears.

Whilst George helped Almer to his feet and out of the cell area, Finnis explained the situation to Alysander.

"Thanks to William, Robert is convinced ye had absolutely nothin' to do with Delmar Wilgart's death."

While Alysander was relieved to hear that bit of news, he still worried over Moirra. No matter how badly she had hurt him by going to Thomas McGregor. "And Moirra?" he asked, his voice cracking ever so slightly.

Finnis's expression turned even more serious before he answered. "Again, ye can thank William here, Robert holds the same opinion fer Moirra."

Relief washed over Alysander, his shoulders sagging as he let loose the breath he'd been holding. "I do no' ken how ye did it, William, but I be grateful to ye."

William grunted. "I rode like the devil with Bruce and Alec, sacrificed food, sleep, and the warmth and love of me wife for more than a fortnight, to go to Stirling and meet with Robert," he told Alysander as if this was something he did every week but hated doing it. "Ye can thank me later, fer now, I need to see me wife. And I swear to ye, Alysander, if ye made me miss the birth of me second child, there will be nowhere safe fer ye to hide from Joanna's wrath."

Alysander chuckled as he gave William a friendly slap on his shoulder. "Then be gone with ye, man!"

William gave a nod to the men and hurried out of the room.

Alysander turned his attention back to Finnis. "Me friend, I could live a thousand life-times and never be able to repay ye fer what ye've done."

"I ken," Finnis said matter-of-factly. "Add this to the long list of debts ye owe me."

Finnis only spoke the truth, therefore Alysander could not argue with him.

Connor clapped his hands together excitedly. "Let us away this godforsaken place and go get that bonny wife of yers."

Any lightheartedness Alysander might have been feeling evaporated instantly. "Nay, Connor, we can no' do that."

A look of astonishment fell over both Connor's and Finnis's faces. "What the bloody hell do ye mean we can no' do that?" Connor asked.

Believing there was no way to hide the truth, Alsyander said, "There be much ye do no' ken, Connor. Moirra be at Thomas McGregor's home as we speak. He tells me she has decided to break our handfast and marry him."

"Have ye lost yer mind?" Finnis asked in stunned disbelief.

"Nay, I have no'," Alysander growled back. "She does no' want me any more. She has made her decision and I'll no' go chasin' after a woman who does no' want me."

'Twas in that small, tiny moment of time, that Finnis Malcolm lost control of all the anger he'd been keeping tamped down and hidden. Drawing back his hand, he rammed his fist into Alysander Malcolm's face, knocking him down to the stone floor.

"Ye are a bloody fool!"

For nearly quarter of an hour, Alysander remained seated on the stone floor, his nose and face throbbing while he listened to both his friend and his brother go on and on about the soundness of his mind and the fact that God had never placed a bigger fool on His earth than the likes of Alysander. "I have never even met yer wife and I ken yer a foolferthrowin' her away on the word of one man!" Connor told him as he furiously paced across the floor.

"I *have* met her, albeit she was quite ill at the time. But I've talked to enough people to ken that Connor be right. Good God, Alysander! Ye are an exasperatin' fool!"

Finally, Alysander was able to ask a question. "Then why be she in Thomas McGregor's home?"

Finnis stood dumbfounded by the question. "Where else was she to go? Do ye no' remember the state of distress she was in when she left here those weeks ago? 'Tis by God's own hand that she has lived, ye fool. They took her to the McGregor home because that be where Deirdre lives. What did ye want them to do, take her to what was left of yer home? Make her sleep in the cold barn while she tries to heal and get better?"

Alysander hadn't thought of that before. Soon, his face felt warm and he ashamedly had to admit that Finnis was right. A heartbeat later, he said, "If I ever get the chance to kill Thomas McGregor, I will take it."

TWENTY-ONE

As soon as Harry learned that Alysander McCullum was being freed, he slid out the back entrance of the gaol and raced to the stables to retrieve his horse. Though honestly, he did not like Thomas, the man was always good for a bottle of whisky or a silver coin for a good deed done well. Harry knew Thomas would want to know as soon as possible that Alysander had been freed by order of Robert II. Mayhap the news was worthy of more than a bottle of whisky or a silver coin.

Either way, no matter how Thomas might reward him, he headed out of town as fast as he could to the McGregor home. News often spread like fire in these parts and he wanted to be certain he was the first to tell him.

Alysander felt all kinds of a fool as he left gaol with Connor and Finnis. In a moment of weakness, he had allowed Thomas McGregor to convince him that Moirra no longer wanted to remain with him. He'd allowed doubt and fear to overrule his common sense. He could blame his lack of intelligence on being locked away for weeks. He might also blame it on the fact that he was overwrought with worry over Moirra and their daughters.

But truth be told, he was simply a man. A man who still felt, at times, wholly inadequate and unworthy.

As he stepped out into the first light of day he'd seen in weeks, the brightness of the sun burned at his eyes. Shielding them with one hand, he stood just outside the gaol, waiting for his eyes to finally adjust. Once they did, he looked out to the streets of Glenkirby.

"What the …" He was taken aback by the sight of at least one hundred, if not more, McCullum men and their mounts. The streets had been flooded, quite literally, with these brave warriors that Alysander had not seen in close to a year.

"I brought reinforcements," Connor said as he stepped toward his horse and took the reins from one of his men. "I like to be prepared."

"Did ye think ye were goin' to war?" Alysander asked.

Connor put one foot in a stirrup and hoisted himself onto his mount. "I did no' ken what to expect, brother. But I knew I was no' leavin' this bloody town without ye." He gave a nod to another warrior, who stepped forward and handed Alysander the reins to a large, black gelding.

Alysander snorted in disbelief. "And ye say Da thought me the most intelligent?" he mumbled under his breath as he mounted the steed.

"Where be ye goin' now?" Finnis asked from the steps.

Alysander smiled as he answered. "To get me wife."

Finnis nodded in agreement. "Mayhap ye should think about bathin' first?"

Connor agreed. "Aye. Ye smell like ye've been sleepin' in yer own shite and filth."

"I have," Alysander said. "There be a wee loch between me home and the McGregor's. I shall bathe there."

Connor tapped the flanks of his horse as the rest of the McCullum men mounted their horses. "How far be that?" Connor asked.

"No' far."

"Good, but mayhap ye could ride at the back. Keep yer smell down wind of us. I fear yer scarin' the horses."

Alysander laughed heartily at his brother. For the first time in weeks, he felt hopeful and alive. "We would no' want to scare yer mount, would we. Lord knows ye have difficulties keepin' yer seat on a tame horse."

Connor rolled his eyes, ignored him, and took off to lead the small army of men out of the village.

Alysander had yet to discover how his brother had come to know he was here, or what the changes were that he had spoken of earlier. He supposed that after he bathed and changed his clothes, his brother might be more apt to have that much needed discussion.

As they neared the small farm Alysander had called home these past months, he galloped to the head of the army to lead the way. Autumn was settling across the land, the air crisp but clear and bright. A day like this made a man feel glad to be alive. The leaves were just beginning to turn from the vivid, lush green he remembered from weeks ago. It would not be long before the land would be an explosion of vibrant colors before turning to the sleepy whites of winter.

Soon, they were pouring into the small courtyard. As soon as Alysander caught sight of the unfinished cottage, he felt guilty. He had been so consumed with worry over Moirra that he had not finished putting on a new thatched roof. An eery silence fell over the little farm as he dismounted.

No chickens scratched at the earth, no sheep bleated or grazed on the nearby hill. No barking dog, no children's laughter clinging to the air. The entire space had been abandoned. Everything was brown and lifeless. Weeds had overtaken the small garden next to the cottage.

And the fields they had worked so hard to plant and had tended with such loving care? Useless now. The barley had gone to seed.

What had he expected? Everything to be exactly as it had been? With Moirra singing while she did the wash? Esa and Orabilis chasing rabbits from the garden? Mariote and Murielle baking bread?

'Twas a sad sight indeed and left him feeling melancholy with longing.

He slid from his horse and went inside the barn that had served as their makeshift home after the cottage had caught fire. Not only was his horse gone, but so was the milking cow and nearly all that remained of their belongings. He searched through the small stall and was glad to see the pallet along with a pack of clean clothes had been left behind. Everything else, from the blankets to the pillows to Moirra's things, was gone.

He grabbed the pack, flung it over his shoulder and left the barn. Connor's face bore an expression of sadness, as if he could feel the pain that stabbed at Alysander's heart.

"The loch be no' far," Alysander said as he mounted his horse.

Connor remained silent as he and his men followed his brother out of the small yard and toward the loch.

TWENTY-TWO

For the first time in many days, Moirra felt strong enough to leave the bed, though she'd not gone far. Deirdre had helped her bathe, don warm woolens and a clean shift, before leaving her alone. Moirra wrapped a shawl around her shoulders that Deirdre had given her earlier, and padded to the tiny window. Pulling away the fur, she rested her head against the sill and stared out at the landscape below.

Where was Alysander?

She knew Thomas had lied to her yesterday. Mayhap not all of what he had said was a untruth, but a good majority of it was. So this morning, when Deirdre had come to help her, Moirra had asked what, if anything, she knew of Alysander's whereabouts. *"As far as I ken, he is still in gaol."*

For reasons she couldn't quite fathom, she took comfort in knowing Alysander was still behind bars, but only because that meant he couldn't leave her. 'Twas probably wrong for her to think such a thing, but at the moment, she cared not about proper thoughts.

Her deepest worry was how he would respond once he learned she had lost the babe. Would he leave her then? Was that the only morsel of truth in Thomas' words? Mayhap the loss would be too much for Alysander. Mayhap that would be the one thing that would send him back into the arms of his family and not hers.

There was no doubt in her heart that Alysander loved her. The only lingering question was, did he love her enough to stay? Did he love her enough to remain on their little farm? Was his love for her stronger than the hatred the townspeople held toward her?

In her heart of hearts she did not think she had the right to ask him to stay, to live out the rest of their life under such scrutiny and shame. The farm itself no longer mattered. She would give it all up in the time it took a heart to beat but once. But where else did she have to go? The farm was all she had left in this world, besides her four daughters. After that, she had nothing.

Alysander had options, far more than she. He could go back to his family, he could go anywhere his heart desired simply because he was a man. As a woman, she did not possess such luxury. As a mother, she had too many people who needed her and counted on her for their very existence.

What kind of life lay ahead for them? Even if Thomas was correct and Alysander was set free, what of her? Was Almer at this very moment on his way to arrest her again for Delmar's murder? She couldn't bear the thought of going through that hell-on-earth again.

There were far too many unanswered questions to make any kind of decision about the future. Knowing that left her feeling even more despondent. How could she plan her future when she did not know from one moment to the next what would become of her this very day?

For the briefest moment, she contemplated taking her own life. She could leave behind a note confessing that she had in fact killed Delmar and could not bear living with the guilt any longer. That would certainly solve a multitude of problems. Her daughters could move on with their lives without fear lingering over their every waking moment. Alysander could go back to his clan and find a woman who had far fewer troubles.

The only thing that stopped her from tying a rope around her neck was imagining what her mother would have thought of such a coward's way out. That and knowing if she took her own life she would spend the rest of eternity rotting in hell. Never again, either in this world or the next, would she rest her eyes upon her beautiful children or Alysander.

She was stuck in a proverbial quagmire of troubles and there was no hope in sight.

Alysander, Connor and the rest of the men thundered across the hills toward the McGregor home. Alysander felt better after having scrubbed away the weeks of filth, shaving his face, and washing his hair. It felt good to don a clean tunic and trews. Refreshed and with a lighter heart, he led the charge. He was a man on a mission. He was going to get his wife and children back.

They were very near the McGregor home when Connor called for a stop with a raised hand. "Brother, I wonder, should we take *all* the men to retrieve yer wife, or just a few?"

Alysander looked at the massive number of men on horseback. While he would certainly take delight in scaring the bloody hell out of Thomas McGregor, he couldn't say he wished to visit the same fear upon the other inhabitants. "Mayhap just a few," he agreed. "But keep the others within shoutin' distance, just in case we need them."

Connor gave the order, pulled ten men from the line, and in no time, they were approaching the McGregor home. It lay in a bowl of sorts, surrounded on all sides by hills of varying sizes. They paused briefly at the top of the hill and looked below. From this vantage point, Alysander could just make out Orabilis and Esa playing out of doors with Wulver. God, how he missed them! Even Wulver, the mutt Orabilis so dearly loved.

They were about to descend the hill when Connor and Alysander spotted two men on horseback heading toward them from the farm below. After a few moments, Alysander could see that it was Thomas McGregor and the fool gaoler, Harry.

"Caution, brother," Alysander warned. "Yer about to meet the biggest horse's arse in all of Scotland."

Connor gave a shrug of his shoulders. "But there be only two of them."

"Aye, but I trust Thomas McGregor about as far as I could throw him."

Alysander, Connor and the ten McCullum warriors did not have to wait long before Thomas and Harry thundered up the hill. They were on full alert, ready for whatever the two men might do.

Thomas did not look the least bit surprised to see Alysander. "What do ye want, McCullum?" he asked as he reined in his mount.

"I've come fer me wife and children."

Thomas chuckled. "Ye can have the children, but yer wife stays with me. As I told ye last night, she is mine now. She wants nothin' to do with ye."

Alysander knew Thomas was baiting him. He wasn't biting. "She can tell me that herself, McGregor. Now stand aside."

"I do no' think so, McCullum. And if ye try to fight yer way through, ye'll find that Almer and at least twenty other men are on their way here as we speak. I'll have ye thrown off me property and arrested fer trespassin'."

"Twenty, ye say?" Connor asked as if he were giving the information some weight.

"Aye," Thomas said with a sneer. "At least twenty. Ye'll be no match fer them."

Connor chewed on it for a brief moment before looking at Alysander. "Mayhap we should turn back, brother."

Alysander smiled. "But it be only twenty more men, Connor."

"True, but it will no' be much of a fight will it?"

Alysander pretended to mull it over. "Probably no'."

Thomas smiled. "Now ye be thinkin' like a smart man, Alysander. Turn away now and we shall let ye live another day."

Alysander raised one brow. "Och! Ye thought I meant 'twould no' be much of a fight fer *yer* men."

Confusion washed over Thomas' face. Before he could ask his next question, Connor gave out a loud whistle. Almost instantly, the ground shook with the reverberation of more than one hundred horses. It rattled the ground as the McCullum men thundered up the hill and spread out behind Connor and Alysander.

A broad smile broke out on Alysander's face as a look of utter astonishment broke out on Thomas' and Harry's.

"Let me clarify it fer ye, McGregor," Alysander said. "I meant 'twould be no' much of a fight fer *us*."

It took a long moment for Thomas to realize he was sorely outnumbered, but he was not quite ready to admit defeat. "She does no' want ye," he ground out.

"I do no' believe ye," Alysander said, his voice firm and unyielding.

Thomas looked out at the hundred men who were slowly making their way down the hill. "Yer a bloody bastard, McCullum!" he ground out.

"I would have to agree with ye," Alysander said as he pushed his way past a very angry Thomas McGregor.

As she contemplated all the things that could go wrong and how to address them, there was a gentle tapping at her door. Believing it was Deirdre coming to check on her for what seemed the hundredth time today, Moirra let out a long heavy sigh. Without taking her eyes off the landscape, she spoke over her shoulder. "I be fine, Deirdre, please, leave me be."

"Ne'er again, lass."

Moirra spun around so quickly at the sound of Alysander's voice that she felt momentarily dizzy from it. Were her eyes playing tricks? Was he truly standing in the doorway?

Every fiber of her being screamed to run to him and fling herself into his arms. But she loved him too much. Catching herself before she could take another step toward him, she pulled the shawl more tightly around her shoulders. "Alysander," she said, nearly choking on impending tears.

His smile was bright, bright enough to light up the darkest of nights. He seemed genuinely happy to see her, which made what she needed to tell him all the more difficult.

The longer they stood looking at one another, the more the smile faded from Alysander's face. Moirra was frozen with fear and trepidation.

"Moirra?" Alysander said her name as he took a tentative step toward her. "Are ye well?"

All she could manage was a rapid nod as she fought to maintain a hold on the tears. If she began crying again, she would not stop, would not be able to give him the freedom to leave.

"Are ye no' happy to see me?" he asked with just a slight tremble to his voice as if he feared her answer.

Another set of rapid nods as she held her breath. Her resolve was waning, fading rapidly.

"Is what Thomas tells me true?"

She had no earthly idea what Thomas had told him.

Alysander took another step toward her. "Do ye no' want me any longer?"

The expression of deep sadness and fear on his face was enough to bring her to her knees. Had he not been standing there to catch her, she would have fallen to the ground.

Wrapping his arms around her, he drew her to his chest. "Moirra, my God how I have missed ye."

Words were lodged in her throat but the tears felt it quite appropriate now to let themselves loose. God above, it felt so good to be in his arms once again. She clung to him with all her might, shaking as she cried and sobbed against his chest. Never did she want to be away from him again. Still, guilt reared its ugly head. How could she ask him to stay?

Repeatedly, he kissed the top of her head and told her he loved her, that he missed her. Each kiss, each term of endearment made her guilt over wanting him grow by leaps and bounds. But as yet, she could not dislodge the lump in her throat or stop the tears from falling long enough to tell him she was going to give him his freedom.

After some time, the tears ebbed, but not his embrace. "I have good news, Moirra. Robert II has found each of us innocent of Delmar's murder. Neither one of us will be hangin' fer it." He whispered the words into her hair as he patted her back. "Moirra, I feared I was goin' to lose ye. When I thought ye did no' want me anymore, it nearly did me in. I can no' imagine me life without ye, without our daughters, without our babe."

'Twas his last words that completely did her in. *Their babe.* The babe she had lost. It mattered not that Robert had declared them innocent, she had lost their babe.

"Moirra, why do ye carry on so? Are ye no happy that we no longer have to worry about being dragged to the gallows?"

Aye, she was glad to hear that, but it mattered not. "Alysander," she choked out. "I lost our babe."

'Twas all he could do to remain standing.

She had lost it, more likely than not due to the horrible conditions she'd been forced to live in for weeks. 'Twas all his fault. Had he thought to confess sooner, this would be a most joyous occasion. For the first time in his adult life, tears filled his eyes. It took a moment before he found his voice. "Moirra, I be so terribly sorry."

She wiped her tears on his tunic before looking up at him. "Why are ye sorry? 'Tis me fault we lost the babe."

"Nay!" he exclaimed. "The fault be mine, lass! Had I confessed sooner, ye'd not have suffered as ye did."

Moirra shook her head. "Nay, 'tis me own fault fer handfastin' with Delmar Wilgart in the first place."

"Nay, Moirra, the fault lies on my head and no one else's," he argued.

Deirdre's voice broke through just then. "Stop it now, the both of ye," she said as she stepped into the room. "The only person to blame is Almer Wilgart. Had he no' been so filled with hatred for Moirra, he would no' have made such horrible accusations against ye or arrested ye. Nay, neither one of ye are to blame fer what has happened and I swear, if I hear either one of ye blame yerselves again, I will whack yer heads together."

Alysander and Moirra stared at her for long moments, each of them afraid to speak their minds.

"Moirra should be able to have more children, though I would recommend ye start on that soon fer we all ken she be no' gettin' any younger."

Moirra thought to argue that point but decided against it. She *was* getting older, as much as it vexed her to admit it. But she was no' quite ready yet to consign herself to sit beside the hearth and carry on on like an auld woman waiting for the good Lord to call her home.

Alysander finally broke the silence that had fallen across the room. "Thank ye, Deirdre, fer takin' such good care of me wife. I will never be able to repay ye."

Deirdre shrugged slightly before commenting. "Moirra is the closest thing to a sister I've ever had. I did what she would have done fer me were our roles reversed."

"I thank ye, all the same," Alysander said, offering her a warm smile. He turned his attention back to his beautiful Moirra. "I love ye, Moirra, with all that I am."

"I love ye as well, Alysander," she replied.

"Do ye feel up to traveling yet?" he asked.

Moirra's brow scrunched in confusion. "Back to our farm?" she asked, feeling the courage rising to argue against that.

"Nay," Alysander said. "Though I loved the life we lived on our wee little farm, Moirra, I fear after all that has transpired these past weeks, we can never go back to living that way again."

She cocked her head to one side, uncertain where he was heading or if he wanted to take her with him.

"Glenkirby has no' been kind to us, Moirra. And even though Robert has found us innocent, I worry about our childrens' futures."

"What are ye suggestin' then?" she asked, uncertain if she was going to like his answer.

He cleared his throat once before answering. "Me brother Connor waits fer us out of doors. Finnis had written to him that I was in more than just a wee bit of trouble, ye see. So he came to help."

She was growing more and more confused. "But I thought yer family ostracized ye after Hugh's death?"

"Well, that was more me da's doin' than me brothers'. They did no' want me to leave, but I was too drunk and too overwrought with guilt to see the truth. Connor has asked me—us—to return to clan McCullum with him."

"But what of yer father, Alysander? I fear I would no' be able to keep quiet if he treated ye as poorly as he has in the past."

Alysander chuckled at her honesty as well as the image of Moirra wagging her finger at his father and putting him in his place. His amusement was short lived when he remembered what he had experienced. "Me father had an apoplexy weeks ago, Moirra. He died a few days later."

Moirra's expression changed to a blend of surprise and sadness. "Och! Alysander, I be so terribly sorry!"

"Do no' worry it much, Moirra. What is done is done."

What Moirra had seen as a completely hopeless life only moments before he walked into the small chamber, was now a future filled with endless possibilities. Still, she had to be certain this was what he truly wanted. "Are ye certain ye want us to continue with our handfastin'? That ye want to raise me daughters as yer own? With yer clan?"

His brow furrowed, his demeanor grew quite serious. "Nay, I be no' talkin' about continuin' with a handfastin', Moirra. I want ye to be me wife. And aye, they be *our* daughters and we shall raise them together. Amongst me clan, or anywhere else on God's earth ye wish to go. As long as we are married, together as a family and away from Glenkirby, I care no' where we live."

Her heart swelled with pride and joy and an overwhelming sense of adoration for this man. She didn't think it possible to love him more than she already had. Wrapping her arms around his waist, she pressed her head against his chest. "As long as we are together, Alysander McCullum, nothin' else matters."

TWENTY-THREE

Thomas McGregor was beyond furious. He had ridden over the crest of the hill, away from all the McCullum warriors and out of their line of vision. Riding into a small copse of trees, he and Harry hid and watched as Alysander McCullum entered the yard. Moirra's brats caught sight of him and ran to him with outspread arms. Alysander wrapped them in a tight hug—those brats who had been nothing less than a nuisances since their arrival—and kissed each of them on the top of their dimwitted heads. 'Twas a reunion that made Thomas' head ache. After several moments of fawning over one another, Alysander entered Thomas' home.

All he had tried to do, the vengeance he had tried to exact from the woman he firmly believed had destroyed his life, was for naught. By now, Moirra was probably in Alysander's arms. It wouldn't take long for the two of them to figure out that Thomas had lied to both.

With countless McCullum warriors either watching his home from a distance or sitting atop their steeds in his yard, there was no hope for him to get to Alysander or Moirra. There was no chance for him to take either of their lives. Hope to ending the years of frustration was gone. Just. Like. That.

"What are ye goin' to do now?" Harry asked.

Thomas shot him an angry glare, quite tempted to take the fool's life. Instead, he remained silent and turned away to stare across the small glen at his cottage. What was he to do now? How would he ever get the revenge he had longed for all these years? More likely than not, Alysander and Moirra were making plans at this very moment to leave, mayhap even to return to her little farm. Who knew what the two of them had in mind.

Just as quickly as his hope had faded, it sprung to life again, when he caught site of something in the yard below. A flash of blue fabric, a dark braid and a flea ridden mutt chasing one another around the area just to the east of his barn.

Orabilis.

Thomas kept a watchful eye on Moirra's youngest daughter as she frolicked and played with her dog. They were not more than one hundred yards away from him. But if he tried to cross the land from his current position he'd be dead in a matter of moments. That route left him far too exposed and put him out in the open, too easily seen by the McCullum warriors.

However, if he went around the long way and came up from behind his barn, he stood a far better chance at getting to Orabilis without being seen. All he needed to do was get her to the opposite side of the barn, out of the line of vision of the warriors.

"Harry," Thomas whispered as he began to back away, farther into the copse. "I need ye to go to Almer as fast as ye can."

"Almer?" Harry asked curiously.

Thomas held his temper in check. "Aye, Almer. Have him meet me as soon as possible at Moirra's farm. There will be ten sillers in it fer ye."

Harry's eyes grew wide with eager anticipation at the mention of the sillers. He gave several rapid nods before turning his horse around and heading toward Glenkirby.

It had been far easier than Thomas had imagined to get to Orabilis. He had backed completely out of the copse, down a small hill, and was making his way toward the barn, when Wulver bounded down the small hill with Orabilis happily chasing after him.

Thomas had taken cover behind a large rock, held his breath steady as he waited for the dog to run past him. Just as he had anticipated, moments later, Orabilis had come running by. In one fell swoop, he had clamped one hand over the brat's mouth, one around her waist and lifted her off the ground. Instantly, she was kicking and flailing about in a vain attempt to free herself from his grasp.

"Hush, ye brat!" he whispered harshly in her ear. "Or I'll kill yer mangy mutt!"

His threat worked and she immediately gave up.

With Orabilis still in his arms, he went to his horse, grabbed the reins and drew him near a large rock. 'Twasn't easy, but he managed to scurry up the boulder and climb onto his horse. A moment later, he had his horse at a full run, heading away from his farm.

Connor had been watching his newly discovered nieces playing together in the yard. It had not taken long to learn that little Orabilis was just as feisty, just as fierce as Alysander had described her. Within moments after introducing himself to the little girl, he knew that she was, even at the tender age of six, a force of nature unto herself.

The three older girls, while quite sweet and adorable, were not quite so unabashedly bold as their youngest sister. They were far more quiet and reserved. Connor knew it would take some time for them to warm to these strangers, even if those strangers were related to Alysander.

Some time had passed when he noticed Orabilis and her dog were no longer playing in the yard near the barn. Something unsettling began to grow deep in his belly, but he was not quite ready to panic just yet. "Where did Orabilis go off to?" he asked her three sisters.

Soon, they were searching around the yard and barn, calling out her name.

"Sometimes she likes to hide, but no' fer long," Mariote told him as she looked into each of the stalls inside the barn. "Orabilis!" she called out. "Mum needs to see ye."

They were met by eery silence. That was when Mariote's expression changed from calm to concerned. She looked at Connor. "She always comes when we say Mum needs her."

They hurried out of the barn and called for Orabilis once again. Nothing.

"What be going on out here?" Deirdre shouted, appearing from inside the house.

Connor paused in the midst of his growing panic to stare at the tall, lovely, dark-haired woman. He blue gaze met his, and for a moment he could not draw his eyes away.

No more could Deirdre.

Mariote stamped her foot. "Connor McCullum, 'tis Deirdre McGregor. Would ye please stop making cow eyes at each other and *help us find our sister?*

Panic grabbed Connor by the throat. From the expressions on the other girls' faces, he knew they were feeling the same. What was he thinking? He quickly explained the situation to Deirdre, though his voice shook—just a little.

"Alec!" Connor called to one of his men who had taken up sentry on the west side of the farm. "Have ye seen the youngest girl?"

Before Alec could answer, Wulver came racing into the yard, barking loudly. Connor, Deirdre and the girls turned to watch as the dog bounded down the hill. Connor held his breath, hopeful that little Orabilis would be right behind him. When she did not immediately appear, he headed toward the hill and raced up it, all the while praying the little girl was on the other side picking flowers or whatever it was that little girls of six did. Behind him, the dog continued to bark ferociously as the other girls called out for their sister.

He stood at the top of the hill and quickly scanned the area below. Nothing but a boulder and a few bushes. From the expressions on the other girls' faces, he knew they were feeling the same. Thinking that mayhap Orabilis was on the other side of the boulder, he nodded at Deirdre raced down the hill as fast as he could. His heart pounded against his chest, not from exertion but from unadulterated worry over a child he'd only just met an hour ago. And just perhaps, from Deirdre's presence.

When he got to the boulder and raced around it, what he found made his blood run cold.

One tiny blue slipper.

Orabilis was not afraid of Thomas McGregor. She was not afraid of any man, alive or dead. She had her *sgian dubh* tucked safely away inside her dress. If Muriale could use *her sgian dubh* to kill a man, then so could Orabilis.

Once she had seen Wulver running away—and only after Thomas had repeatedly tried to run him over with his horse—she felt better. Thomas had said he'd kill Wulver, not her, so she wasn't truly worried. Besides, once her sisters saw Wulver return without her, they would know something was wrong and would come looking for her. Hopefully they would bring her new uncle, Connor, with them. Not because she needed him to protect her or rescue her from Thomas McGregor. Nay, she simply wanted a grown up there to witness her bravery. She'd wait until Connor or Alysander arrived before she killed Thomas.

Because she wasn't truly afraid, she was able to think clearly, or at least in her own mind it all made sense. Thomas was too focused on getting away from his farm to pay much attention to what she was doing.

All along the way, she left signs for her family to follow. First she dropped her other slipper, then the bits of food she always kept in her pouch for Wulver. Next, after carefully pulling the string from the pouch, she dropped it on the ground. After that she dropped the pouch, then the pretty bit of ribbon she used to bind her braid.

Later, she slipped one toe into the top of her woolens to slide it off. Although she was quite certain where they were headed, she didn't want to drop the next woolen too soon, just in case he surprised her. When she looked ahead and caught sight of their old home, she breathed a sigh of relief, but waited, just in case Thomas was trying to trick her.

Thankfully, he wasn't as smart as he thought he was. He rode his horse into her old yard and dismounted first, before pulling her down. He grabbed a rope from the back of his saddle and headed into her cottage.

Had she been the one doing the kidnapping, she wouldn't have taken her prisoner to a familiar place. Nay, she imagined she would have gone somewhere far away and strange. But then Thomas McGregor was meaner than he was smart. As far as she was concerned, he made a terrible kidnapper.

Once inside the small cottage he glanced around for a spot to tie her to. Realizing what he was doing, Orabilis said, "If I were ye, I'd tie me to the ladder." There really wasn't much left inside the cottage after the fire. Though she and her sisters had cleaned it out, had scrubbed the walls and floors, they had yet to replace any of the furniture.

"Shut up, ye little shite!" he growled at her.

Orabilis shrugged as if she didn't truly care what he was doing. Thomas continued to look around the space. "Ye might also consider the barn," Orabilis said. "There be lots more things to tie me to in there."

"I said to shut up!" he growled again. Soon, he gave up looking for a perfect spot and ended up doing what she had suggested in the first place. Thomas shoved her down onto the floor. He took the rope and looped it around her waist twice before tying it off to the ladder.

Nay, he was not a very good kidnapper at all.

Alysander, Connor, and McCullum warriors were thundering across the countryside in search of Orabilis.

Less than a quarter an hour before, Connor had stormed inside the McGregor home to tell Alysander that his youngest daughter was missing. Moirra went as white as a sheet and nearly fainted from fear while Alysander nearly fell to his knees. With a last, lingering glance at Connor, Deirdre went to Moirra to reassure her. Connor explained things as he knew them to be at that moment, but Alysander didn't need to guess who had Orabilis. He *knew*.

Thomas McGregor.

They left Moirra in the care of her three oldest daughters and twenty of the McCullum warriors to guard them and were soon off in search of Orabilis. With each beat of his heart, his fury grew. Thomas McGregor was proving to be far more than just a liar. He was downright dangerous.

It had been one of their warriors who had first caught sight of the little blue slipper, which was quickly followed by the pouch. By the time they found her woolen, Alysander was certain he knew where Thomas was heading.

"Yer daughter be right smart," Connor shouted over the rumble of hoofbeats.

Alysander was too furious to be proud, or to think of anything but getting to his daughter and ending once and for all, the life of Thomas McGregor. Later, much later, after he had his daughter back and Thomas's head on a pike, he might take a moment to think on how smart she was to leave a trail.

They hadn't replaced the ladder yet, which was good for Orabilis. 'Twas also fortuitous that Thomas was more focused on the impending arrival of Alysander than he was on his captive. He paced back and forth in front of the door, mumbling and muttering incoherently to himself. Only occasionally did he glance at the girl.

He began to seem much different than the Thomas she had known her entire life. The more he paced, the more his eyes changed. She couldn't quite name what was different about them, just that they weren't the same. Soon, those eyes looked glassy, like her mum's had when she was ill with the fever.

That was when Orabilis began to grow afraid, for the first time in a very long time.

Dealing with a stupid man was one thing. Dealing with a man who was stupid *and* dangerous? That was different.

She felt her bravery begin to waiver the more he mumbled and cursed and paced.

How long had they been gone from the farm? Had anyone realized yet that she was missing? Had Wulver gotten back to the McGregor farm? Would they find the trail she had left behind?

Fear grew and grew. It wasn't long before she felt the need to pee, but was too afraid to ask for permission to go out of doors. Nay, the longer they were there, in the tiny cottage, the more frightening Thomas became and the more terrified she became. *Would they ever get here?*

TWENTY-FOUR

No matter how hard she tried, Orabilis couldn't stop a tear from trailing down her cheek. It seemed as though they had been in this cottage for hours and hours. Mayhap no one had realized she was missing. Mayhap Thomas was going to lose his mind waiting for them. Mayhap he would kill her before anyone got here to rescue her.

'Twas still daylight so mayhap they hadn't been here as long as it felt like, but she was certain that they had been here a very long time. Her stomach hurt, from worry as much as needing to pee. If she didn't get out soon, she was going to make a mess on the floor.

She was trying to muster the courage to ask to go outside when she thought she heard thunder rumbling in the distance. Thomas heard it too, for his head perked up and he stepped out the door and looked off to the west. A moment later, he darted by inside and was hovering over her, his eyes dark and glassy. "If ye so much as utter a single sound, I will cut yer throat from ear to ear!" he whispered, his voice harsh and menacing.

Orabilis nodded rapidly in affirmation.

Thomas left her there and went outside, closing the door behind him.

The moment he left, she felt some of her bravery return.

Thomas was standing just outside the door to the cottage when Alysander, Connor and the others came racing into the yard. He didn't so much as move a muscle as the yard quickly filled with angry McCullum men.

"Where is she?" Alysander yelled as he dismounted and headed toward Thomas.

"Where be who?" Thomas asked, feigning ignorance.

Alysander stopped just a few feet away, the vein in his neck throbbing as he unsheathed his sword. "Ye ken bloody well who! Orabilis!"

"I've no' seen her since I left me farm earlier," Thomas told him.

"Ye lie, McGregor. Ye took her. Where is she?"

"I told ye I do no ken where she be. Mayhap Almer Wilgart took her," Thomas said, trying hard to act as if he truly didn't know.

Alysander paused as he studied Thomas closely. He hadn't even considered the possibility of Almer taking Orabilis.

Behind him, Connor and a few dozen men dismounted and began spreading out across the yard. Some of them went into the barn to search for the child.

"We all ken Almer be no' of sound mind," Thomas suggested. "Mayhap he took her to get back at ye and Moirra. Who kens what a man like that will do."

Something in Thomas' demeanor, something about the look in his eyes, told Alysander that the man knew more than he was letting on. While there was a distinct possibility that Almer had Orabilis, it was just as likely Thomas was involved.

"She is no' in the barn!" someone called out from behind him.

Alysander continued to study Thomas, not taking his eyes off him for even the briefest moment.

"Step aside, McGregor," Alysander ordered.

Thomas shrugged his shoulders and took a few short steps to the side. Thomas still had his sword sheathed but that didn't mean he could be trusted. Alysander hurried toward the door and flung it open. Just before he stepped inside, Thomas McGregor lunged at him, shoving him inside the cottage and to the floor. The wind was momentarily knocked from Alysander's lungs when he landed face first, with Thomas on his back.

As soon as Thomas had shut the door behind him, Orabilis was able to wiggle her way out of the rope. With no idea what Thomas had planned, she had scrambled to the other side of the room and hidden herself as best she could behind the door. She was able to hear Alysander and Thomas quite clearly and when Alysander ordered Thomas to step aside, she scooted farther away, for she didn't want the door to crash into her.

Then she saw Alysander fly into the room, face down, with Thomas on his back. When she saw the flash of metal in Thomas' hand, she acted quickly and without much thought. With her hand wrapped tightly around her *sgian dubh,* she stood and flung herself onto Thomas' back and plunged the blade into his shoulder with all her might.

Thomas let out a scream before tossing her off his back. She landed hard, banging her head against the stone floor. The pain was instant and dizzying. Quite suddenly, everything around her grew fuzzy and distorted, then black.

As soon as Connor realized what was happening, he bounded into the cottage, his sword drawn and at the ready. He was about to plunge it into Thomas' back when Orabilis flew from behind the door. He couldn't very well do anything but watch as she thrust her little *sgian dubh* into Thomas' shoulder. But as soon as Thomas threw her off and sat up to bury his own blade in Alysander, Connor could finally react.

His blade hit its mark, just under Thomas' right shoulder blade. It tore through skin, flesh, and muscle, scraping against a bit of bone, before making its way through and out his chest. Blood trickled down his back and a moment later, when Connor removed the blade, blood began to pour. A heartbeat later, Thomas slowly fell sideways onto the floor.

Thomas McGregor was dead.

EPILOGUE

Almer Wilgart was unwilling to bring charges against Connor McCullum for the death of Thomas McGregor. With more than one hundred witnesses—many of whom threatened to slice him into tiny bits of flesh to feed to scavengers—how could he? The only thing that brought him any amount of satisfaction was knowing that as soon as Moirra and Orabilis were well enough to travel, the whole lot of them would be departing Glenkirby forever.

Due to their strong desire to leave, it took less than a day for Deirdre to declare both Moirra and Orabilis fit for travel. At Connor's kind invitation, Deirdre agreed to go north with them, under the pretense that Moirra or Orabilis might still need her. Alysander thought mayhap it had to do more with the way Connor and Deirdre kept looking at one another when they thought the other wasn't looking. A romance was rapidly blossoming between the two, even if they were not quite yet ready to admit it.

William, James and Phillip were now left with all the McGregor lands, as well as Moirra's after she agreed to sell it to them at a fair price. Though they were sad to see her and her daughters leave, they were even more reluctant to have their only blood sister go as well. Each man made open promises that if anything happened to Deirdre, there would not be a safe place on God's earth for anyone to hide from their wrath. There wasn't a man among the McCullum's who didn't believe them.

It took ten days of slow riding before they finally arrived at the McCullum keep. Although Alysander had Connor's word that the only person who held any sort of ill-feelings against him for Hugh's death was dead, "Unless ye want to count all the hearts ye broke whilst ye were here," Connor teased, "ye needn't worry."

Alysander was still leery about his return. The moment they crossed the small creek that divided the keep from the glen, his unease increased tenfold.

Moirra, who had ridden the entire journey in front of him, with his arms wrapped protectively around her, could feel his tension rising. "Remember, Alysander, things are no' as they once were. Besides, ye have me and Orabilis to protect ye," she jested. Somehow, that did lighten his apprehension.

The clan came out to cheer the safe return of their men. The courtyard was filled with McCullum clansmen, women and children, all smiling and cheering openly. Alysander believed their happy greeting was meant more for Connor and the other men than he and his new family.

Archibald, his second eldest brother, was there to greet them all as well, though in truth, he was mightily surprised to see Alysander. After dismounting, Alysander kept a protective arm around his wife as he offered a guarded smile to his brother.

Archibald was having none of it. A clearly relieved and joyful smile erupted on his face as he wrapped his arms around Alysander and lifted him off his feet. "Och! I thought I'd never lay me eyes on yer sorry hide again, brother!"

Archibald, who never really understood his own strength, nearly squeezed the life out of Alysander. After several long moments, he finally sat his brother back on his feet and looked him up and down. "Yer sober?" he said with the most confused expression on his face.

Alysander's face burned red for a moment. "Aye, I be sober. Have been for months now."

Archibald raised a disbelieving brow as he scratched his beard covered jaw. "Months?"

"Aye, months."

"Be it a woman?" Archibald asked.

Alysander laughed heartily at his brother's keen assessment. "In truth, it be five women."

Archibald's eyes nearly bulged from their sockets. "Ye've a harem?"

Alysander smiled slyly and shook his head. "Nay, I've a wife and four daughters," he said as he stepped back to his wife and motioned for their daughters to come forward.

Archibald stared in utter disbelief at the sight before him. Alysander McCullum, not only married, but appearing quite happy about it, and now the father of four daughters.

Alysander, Moirra, and her daughters settled into life at the McCullum keep with only a few minor hiccups. The first being when Orabilis discovered the armory. The second being when Mariote became smitten with one of the warriors. But all in all, their first week at the keep was a whirlwind of excitement and relief.

Archibald would often catch sight of his brother and bonny Moirra together, all a twitter and blissfully happy. He still couldn't quite believe his drunkard of a brother, the one they thought would die in a drunken brawl before he ever took a wife, was now happily married. On several of those occasions, Archibald would declare, "Ye? Married? With four daughters?" he shook his head, as if he were still unable to wrap his head around the news. "Next ye'll be tellin' me the bloody English have set David free!"

A week later, they received two letters. The first from William McGregor letting his sister ken that Joanna had delivered another boy. He was quite healthy and possessed a good set of lungs. They named him Alysander.

The second missive was from Finnis Malcolm.

We have just received most glorious news. At the time I write this letter to ye, our beloved King is on his way to Stirling Castle.

The English have finally set him free.

AFTERWARD

Most of my readers know that I have never typed 'The End' to any of my stories. *Saving Moirra's Heart* will not be an exception. Yes, I do plan on writing more about Alysander, Moirra and their four daughters. However, there are several other stories that I must finish first. I hope to return to Alysander and Moirra in 2017.

OTHER BOOKS BY SUZAN TISDALE

The Clan MacDougall Series
Laiden's Daughter
Findley's Lass
Wee William's Woman
McKenna's Honor

The Clan Graham Series
Rowan's Lady
Frederick's Queen

The Clan McDunnah Series
Caelen's Wife - Book One: A Murmur of Providence
Caelen's Wife - Book Two - A Whisper of Fate
Caelen's Wife - Book Three - A Breath of Promise

Moirra's Heart Series
Stealing Moirra's Heart
Saving Moirra's Heart

With Dreams Only Of You
The Legend of the Theodosia Sword, arriving in 2015

ABOUT THE AUTHOR

Suzan lives in the Midwest with her verra handsome carpenter husband and the youngest of their four children. They are currently accepting monetary donations to help feed their 17-year-old, 6'3", built-like-a-linebacker son.

They live in a quiet little hamlet where the only traffic jams are caused in the very early morning hours when they have to wait for the wild deer and turkeys to cross the road.

Stay up to date:
www.suzantisdale.com
twitter@suzantisdale
Facebook: suzantisdaleromance
Email: suzan@suzantisdale.com